Shantyboat
American Dystopia

Carl Parsons

Wordwooze Publishing
wordwooze.com

Cover by Margaret Loftin-Whiting

This is a work of fiction. Names, places, characters, and incidents either are the product of the author's imagination or are used fictitiously, and any resemblance to any persons, living or dead, businesses, companies, events, or locales is entirely coincidental.

Per mi si va ne la città dolente ...
[*Through me one enters the sorrowful city ...*]
Inscription above the Gate of Hell
Dante, *Inferno*, 3.1

Chapter 1: Meeting

The floodwall service gate was open. Dale had never seen it open before, didn't even realize there was such a thing. But his days on the streets had left him bored and longing for diversion, so he walked through the gate and began to look around. Before him, a small armada of shantyboats bobbed on the smaller river that emptied into the larger one, the Ohio. Four of the shanties were tied to a makeshift wharf. One other was tied to a small tree that had sprung up along the riverbank since the park that had once been on this location had become neglected. And a sixth one was moored by two lines that were attached to rebars that had been pounded into the riverbank's soft soil. All the shanties were makeshift affairs, constructed from assorted materials, more often than not mismatched, without so much as a coat of paint to harmonize them.

On the floodwall behind Dale, large white commercial letters, made of molded plastic, shouted to the once bustling river "Welcome to Parkeston." Below that message was a smaller one in blue graffiti, stained over time by floodwater and faded by the sun to near obliteration. Still, one could make out the invitation, "Let's be friends."

Fascinated by the scene, Dale squatted down below the blue graffiti in the shade and anonymity of the wild large-leafed shrubbery that had overtaken the park to watch life on the river. Besides, a welcome breeze was blowing across the Ohio River toward him, which brought a bit of relief from the heat and humidity of the streets he was already experiencing on this sweltering summer morning. Moreover, the river scene appealed to him in another way, one he couldn't quite identify yet. It gave him comfort to see people belonging to something, their patchwork shantyboat homes where they slept and ate and reared their children, while he no longer belonged to anything. Perhaps that was it—belonging—that simple, obvious quality about the scene that he couldn't name at first. Perhaps that's all there was to it, belonging, just that.

Content for the moment, he sat, his back against the floodwall, and watched. Watched a woman hanging laundry to dry along a clothesline she'd just fastened in place on the shoreline side of her shantyboat. Watched the children playing, screeching, and running about from shanty to shanty in a game of tag. He wondered what agility kept them from toppling, one after another, into the river, so reckless was their play. Watched a second woman who was scraping the remains of breakfast into the river water from plates stacked on an unpainted wooden bench beside her. Watched still another shanty where a shirtless man in blue dungarees leaned back in a cane chair against the weather-stained plywood siding of his shanty's cabin, propped his bare feet up on a railing, pulled a red canvas ballcap down over his eyes, and seemed to be enjoying for the moment a nap in the morning sun. Watched more children run back and forth along the wharf, which shook precariously under their feet. Heard a woman's voice shouting at them from one of the shanty cabins to stop or else the whole wharf might break and fall into the river and them with it, she said. *From the looks of the wharf,* Dale thought, *she could very well be right.*

Suddenly, he was aware of a presence nearby, its shadow cast obliquely on the ground before him. "May I join you?" the presence asked. "My name's Rodney," it added, omitting its last name, for everyone had become cautious about disclosing information to strangers. "Think I've seen you a time or two at the community canteens."

Dale looked up at the man who was considerably taller than himself, rod-thin and clearly in need of a shave. Rodney's mostly black scruff was patched with grey. He wore a faded denim shirt with tan trousers permanently stained at the knees but otherwise clean. And he stood close enough that Dale could tell his clothes weren't old yet, not street-old, that is, since they lacked the telltale body odor that would come with a week or two of wearing them constantly, day and night, asleep and awake, as most vagrants had to do now, or did anyway when they found clothes that fit them properly. The clothes made Dale wish he had fresher ones himself. He resolved to look for some tonight at one of the community shelters.

"And my name's Dale," he said, rising to shake Rodney's hand. Dale was shorter than Rodney but stockier and much more muscular, his hair dark and curly. "Sure, have a seat. Reserved this one right here just for you!" Dale joked and pointed to a grassy spot beside him. He added, "Yeah, I believe I've seen you around the streets, too. Plenty of us just walk around these days with nothing to do. Kills time and gives you some exercise, if nothing else." Now

2

they both sat on the ground, leaning against the floodwall, while the sun worked its way up the eastern sky to their left.

"I came out here to see why that service gate is open. Don't see any reason for it, though. Do you, Dale?"

"No. And I did the same as you. Came out here 'cause I was curious but not seen a thing yet to explain the gate being open. Nope, sure haven't."

"Say, those shantyboats look like a good idea, don't they?" Rodney said, motioning toward the scrap lumber fleet on the little river. "One of those could at least give a person some privacy, a place he could call his own without the expense of real estate. Got to be better than sleeping in the community shelters every night."

"Yep, I was just thinking the same thing. And gives a person a chance to have a meal of his own choice now and again instead of always standing in line at the community canteens. Why, I just saw a woman slop her family's breakfast plates into the river over there." Dale pointed to one of the shanties tied to the wharf.

"If she does that very often, I'll bet the carp and catfish along here eat well and grow real fat," Rodney laughed, then added in a serious, thoughtful tone, "And more important, I'll bet a shantyboat could help keep a family together, the wife and the kids with the man, as they should be. Not the way it mostly is any more with the families all broken apart, men in one shelter, women and children in another, maybe a mile or more apart."

"Yep, with the way things are today, people can't even afford to stay together. A wife gets more Federation support for her kids if their father's gone. So, most dads are. Lots of them wandering here and there looking for work. The same all over the country, I hear."

"True. In fact, way too true. And it doesn't matter who actually does the leaving, either—the wife or the husband. My wife took our boy and little girl and left me shortly after I lost my job. Went off to her parents over in Columbus. You can just bet she's claiming me as an absent father to get more benefits even though she's the one who did the leaving. Her father has a government pension. Used to be a postmaster in one of the Columbus suburbs. Said he could keep my wife and kids at his place until things improve, if they ever do. But the truth is, I haven't heard from them since they left. I called and sent them letters at first but received no replies. I can't call any more since I lost my phone at one of the shelters. And since I lost our house, also, to foreclosure, she has no way to reply to me now even if she wanted to. So, for now at least, we're lost to each other, which seems to be what she wanted anyway. She's likely found somebody else by this time."

"How long has she been gone?"

"About a year and a half now, maybe a little longer. The only thing I have left from her is this knife." Rodney pulled a large folding knife from his rear pants pocket. "She gave it to me for a birthday present about five years ago. Knives have never been a great interest of mine, but I guess she didn't know what else to buy. Anyhow, as repo men were throwing me out of the house, I took this along with me, mostly for protection, since I knew I was about to become homeless." Rodney handed the knife to Dale for inspection. "It's a six-inch lock-back with an antler bone handle. I've had to show it a time or two in the streets to avoid trouble, so now I'm glad she did buy it and glad I thought to grab it before I left the house. Just good luck that I've been able to hold onto it."

"Sorry, Rodney. Sorry to hear all that." Dale returned the knife after opening and closing it twice, testing its action, and nodding his head approvingly. "Similar thing happened to me, though, about eight months ago. My wife just up and ran off when things got tough for us. Took our two little girls with her. And just like you, I haven't seen or heard from them since." Dale paused a while before adding, "Don't even know for sure where they are. Down toward Charleston, I think. My wife went off with another man, to be honest about it. Leastways, that's what a neighbor told me. Said she saw 'em go. And this ole gal makes a point to know what everybody's up to. Spies on them, so she's probably right. Thought something was up with my wife as things were starting to go downhill with my job and all. Guess I was right to suspect her, not that it did me any good."

"Sorry for you, too, Dale. Lost your house, too, I guess?"

"Sure did. Just like you, Federation-owned bank came on in and took it over soon as I fell behind on the mortgage payments. Didn't give me a chance to find another job, not that I could have. Or to catch up on the payments or do anything else to help save the situation. Not that I could have come up with the money, either. I know I couldn't have. So, they just dumped me out on the street with a few clothes, the same way they're doing with everybody else. Now

4

here I am, out on the streets with nothing to do. That's the worst part for me, I think—having nothing to do but roam around and think about my troubles. Some days I don't even say a word to anybody, just a grunt or two or maybe a head nod to some other poor guy in line at one of the canteens. How 'bout you? Where are you staying now?"

"No one place in particular, just wherever I can. Different shelters here and there around town. Just depends on where I am at the end of the day. None of the shelters are very hospitable any more. They've become so crowded that nobody wants to use them. Not enough of them, it seems, for all the vagrants on the streets now. And whenever it rains or snows, I crouch down inside the nearest doorway I can find opposite the wind until the shelters open again for the night."

Rodney sighed a bit, then added, "These troubles, this Greater Depression as everybody calls it, they've gone on for so long now they seem to have no end in sight. And the Federation pays for all the welfare by just printing up some more money. So, we end up with the worst of all worlds—high prices, poor selection of products, money that's worth next to nothing to buy the junk products from the forced labor factories, and no jobs to earn even the worthless money. All designed to put us at the mercy of the Federation, I think. Plus, it puts everyone on edge, since you never know what disaster will happen to you next, as if not having a family, a home, or a job weren't disaster enough. Also, nobody tells you anything you can rely on. There's no real news, just Federation propaganda."

"Yep, we all have problems these days. Big ones. Takes a bushel full of dollars just to buy yourself a loaf of bread. Can't even remember the last time I had any money to buy my own food. Isn't that what happened to the Germans before Hitler came along, sky-high prices?"

"It is. Put an end to German democracy at the time. The Weimar Republic it was called."

"Thought so, not that I know much about history. Well, unless you've still got a job, you've not got much choice but to fetch your meals in a community canteen, and eat what the Federation chooses to feed you, and end up each day in a community shelter to sleep, and you're supposed to be thankful for it. I'm like you, Rodney, I think that's the way they want it—keep us all poor and ignorant so they can do whatever they want to us." Dale was shaking his head as he spoke. "Never thought it would be like this, not here in America, but here it is. And worse yet, it all came to pass on our watch, and nobody lifted a finger to stop it."

Then the two fell silent, just listening to the squeals and screeches of the children at play, the stomping of their bare feet on the wharf and shanty decks, the monotonous lapping of the river water, and their own anxieties rumbling inside them with the persistence of hunger pangs.

Chapter 2: Prisoners

Before long, Rodney stood up, slowly, cautiously at first, thinking he'd heard something. "Uh-oh, here comes the reason the service gate's open, I'll bet," he said. "Look up that way, Dale." He pointed along the riverbank, upstream, off to the east, into the glare of the morning sun.

In response, Dale rose now, also, and looked, using both hands to shield his eyes. He saw a procession of guards in khaki uniforms, each carrying a shotgun, and with them a group of prisoners, clad in fluorescent orange jumpers. He counted them, ten prisoners in all, bending over, straightening up, then bending down again, all lugging partially filled black plastic bags. Today the prisoners were at work on trash detail, picking up after the vagrants who had littered the riverbank with their discarded meal containers, water bottles, and articles of filthy, worn-out clothing. All left by the army of those who walked the town's streets these days and dwelled along its perimeters, even outside the floodwall, a few of them in shantyboats, like those bobbing before the two men now, all those people not much better off than the trash they had left behind.

And Dale knew that he was just like them, a vagrant now himself. So, too, was Rodney. All the vagrants were linked by misfortunes that had crippled the entire country, misfortunes unique in details to each of them, perhaps, but common to all in their effect. Even so, Dale felt he was at least better off than these prisoners. *They're wearing those dirty orange jumpsuits with the black bullseyes stamped on the front and back,* he thought. *Everyone knows what those bullseyes are for!*

These prisoners had said something or done something to offend the Federated States of America. Or at least somebody claimed that they had. Now they were paying for their crimes, whether real or imagined, with forced labor. These prisoners on the riverbank were working out short-term sentences. Others, in distant labor camps associated with nationalized factories, were serving long-term sentences. Many of the latter, probably most, would eventually pay with their lives. Kept in open pens on clear nights, like livestock, and only allowed into crude barracks for shelter during storms and cold weather, their days of suffering were normally shortened by various illnesses or minor injuries. While often fatal now, these types of injuries to a healthy person in the Happy Times before the Greater Depression would have meant little more than the inconveniences of first aid treatment. But for these prisoners, a simple scratch often became an infection, and an infected wound developed into gangrene. A common head cold caught under the chilling stars became pneumonia. Thus, death, knowing well the labyrinthine ways of life, came to the Federation's prisoners by these varied paths, bringing with it an ironic mercy that ended their sufferings as quickly as it could, to satisfy itself, if nothing else, before moving on to its next victims.

Dale had heard their stories, mostly through rumors in the canteens and shelters, but occasionally from a rare survivor met in the streets, ones sent into exile from their home state and forbidden to return. Their exiles presumably served to warn others they might encounter not to oppose the Federation in any way but always and in all things to conform.

Today, at least, these prisoners weren't dying, but the sun was beginning to bake them along the riverbank, roasting their necks, their shoulders, and their hunched-over backs, bent to the task of cleaning up trash.

"Just look at them, Rodney," Dale said. "A wrong move and those poor bastards could be shot dead by those guards. At least we are better off than they are. We still have the freedom to walk around."

"Yes, but we do our walking in a broken country with no hope of it getting better."

As the prisoners drew closer, Dale and Rodney could hear their rubber sandals slapping against their bare heels. The guards, in contrast, were smartly dressed in blue uniforms and leather boots. Cradled in their arms were double-barreled shotguns. They stalked the prisoners like sheepdogs, watching them closely, ready to snarl and nip and bite if any prisoner moved too far this way or that, even if one of them stood up to stretch his aching back too long.

One of the guards, the one nearest Dale and Rodney, separated himself from the others and began walking toward the shantyboats, moving with a brisk, purposeful walk, and headed straight for the shantyboat tied to the tree. He was holding his shotgun upright against his right shoulder, his forefinger on the trigger guard. As he passed by the first shanty, the man who was sunning himself awoke with a start, jumped to his feet, and ducked inside his cabin like a rabbit into the brush. The guard gave him a glance and laughed aloud, a harsh and derisive laugh, but otherwise continued on. The children on the wharf, when they saw the guard, fell silent and stood stock-still, watching in silence as he walked by while the wharf still throbbed beneath their feet. "Morning, kids," the guard said in a tone little changed from his mocking laughter. The children watched him without answering, then dispersed, running to their various shanties, calling to their parents in anxious voices that told of an ominous presence that they only vaguely understood but acutely sensed.

A woman was standing on the bow of the shanty that was tied to the tree, her two small children, most likely three- and four-year-olds, playing around her. The guard stopped abruptly beside her boat and stared at her.

"Look out, something's going to happen here, I'm afraid," Rodney whispered to Dale as he crouched down behind the shrubs. Dale instinctively knelt beside him.

"What do you think is going to happen?" Dale asked in a hushed voice. He spread apart the branches of the shrubbery in front of him just enough to see the guard, who was still standing beside the shantyboat, about fifty yards away, scowling at the woman.

"Nothing good, I'm thinking," was all Rodney could reply before the guard began to berate the woman in a loud voice.

"Get the hell down here, woman, and pick up this shit like I told you earlier." The guard motioned to the assortment of discarded items beside the shantyboat with the sweep of his left hand while still holding the shotgun erect. "Do it now, you old cow! Do what I told you to do earlier!"

The woman shouted back at him, "Don't you be cursing me like that, not in front of my kids! The fact is, you shouldn't be cursing me at all. I got my rights, too, you know. I need to be respected. Besides, that ain't our trash."

"You got nothin' in the way of rights while you got trash on the ground," the guard shouted back at her. "You got nothin' but trash on this here bank that needs to be picked up. That's all you got. And I'm tellin' you now and for the last time—just like I told you before, when we first got here this morning—to get down here and do it. Pick up this trash right now or else!"

9

"Well, I ain't goin' to! That's what them prisoners are here for. Ain't that why you got them out here today, to pick up trash? So, let them do it. I ain't no prisoner, and that ain't my trash!" As the woman spoke, she thrust both hands outward as though she were casting a spell on the riverbank, its litter, and the guard—a spell that removed all of them from her world.

Unimpressed with the woman's sorcery, the guard leveled the shotgun at her. "I'm tellin' you for the last time, woman. Do as I say and do it right now, or I'll blast you from here to hell. I really will! You been warned and re-warned."

The woman didn't flinch, didn't move at all, in fact, except to jam her fists against her hips and shout back, "Go ahead, big shot. We're already in hell—all of us livin' here—and we been put here by the likes of you. So there!" She emphasized her claim by pointing at the guard, jabbing her forefinger in his direction.

The guard came several steps closer to the woman, now no more than twenty feet from her, and levelled his weapon. The blast of the shotgun tore into her chest, sending out a cloud of flesh and blood and propelling her backward, slamming her into the shanty's door jamb before she fell through the open doorway. Her children, silenced for a moment by shock, began to scream, hunched over their mother's body, imploring her to rise again. Suddenly, a shirtless man thrust his head out the door. "What the hell's goin'—?" He tried to say more, but a second blast from the guard's shotgun ripped open his face and sent him, too, flying backward into the cabin. Splattered with their parents' gore, the children wailed all the more frantically, utter terror seizing them now.

Next the guard untied the shantyboat's mooring lines from the tree. Did it casually and calmly, as though nothing out of the ordinary had happened and he were merely tidying up a small mess. He tossed the lines onto the shanty's deck near the screaming children. Slowly, caught by the small river's current, the shantyboat began to drift from shore, unnoticed at first by the children, consumed as they were with grief for their murdered parents and terror for themselves. The guard watched for a few moments as the shanty drifted away, then, satisfied by his own actions, reloaded his shotgun, pulling two new shells methodically from a black cloth pouch hanging at his side. The spent shells he tossed into a trash bag held by the nearest prisoners.

10

"We need to get the hell out of here!" Dale whispered hoarsely to Rodney, looking at him with eyes widened by shock. "Don't you think we should?"

"We do," Rodney quickly replied, nodding his head, "but not yet. The guards will see us for sure if we make a move right now. They're too close. Let's just stay where we are and be patient. Soon as the prisoners clean up what that woman wouldn't, they'll leave. Then we can go."

"Yeah, but they'll close the service gate behind them when they do go, won't they?"

"That's okay if they do. We'll just have to hike upstream a little way to where the floodwall ends. It's no more than a mile or so. That's better than getting caught as witnesses to a guard's killing of two innocent people and setting their orphans adrift. Then we'd be the ones picking up trash—that is, if we were lucky enough to live that long. Better for us just to watch and wait."

"Okay, but I sure hope you're right."

They fell silent again, hunkered down even more behind the shrubs, concealing themselves as best they could. In the distance they could still hear the cries of the children and could see the shantyboat as it drifted more quickly now into the Ohio. There, the much stronger current of the big river was already carrying the shanty toward the island that lay to the southwest of the town and there split the river into two channels.

For the next twenty minutes or so, the men didn't dare speak, scarcely breathed. Perspiration oozed from them as they watched the prisoners continue to pick their way along the riverbank, gradually coming closer and closer. The prisoners were careful not to look in the direction of the drifting shantyboat, even though they couldn't help but hear the children's cries reverberating up the river valley. But they didn't dare show that they heard or saw anything. Finally, all of them, both prisoners and guards, converged in the shade of the tree where the shanty had been tied. There the prisoners methodically bagged the trash that the murdered woman had refused to gather.

While they worked, a guard spoke to one prisoner and made vague gestures toward the shrubs where Dale and Rodney were hiding. Some litter had blown up that way. *Go get it*, the guard seemed to be saying to the prisoner through his determined gestures.

11

When the prisoner, clutching his trash bag, came close enough, he could see the men through the gaps in the shrubbery. Recognizing this, Rodney quickly raised his forefinger to his lips, staring at the prisoner desperately. The man gave a slight but perceptible nod, gathered up the trash, and then, without saying anything or looking back, rejoined the others who were already trooping off toward the service gate. Two guards walked ahead of them, and three others, including the killer, brought up the rear. When all the prisoners had passed through the gate, two of the guards swung it closed. It settled into place behind them with a heavy dull thud, sealing the city off from the river, the shantyboats, and the murders.

Dale and Rodney immediately broke from their cover and stood staring at each other, greatly relieved at their own fate yet greatly troubled by the fate of the orphans. Both turned to look, almost simultaneously but silently, down the long river valley where the shantyboat bearing two bloodied, shot-riddled bodies and the two orphaned children floated toward the east channel of the big island. By now the shanty had shrunk to not much more than a blackish dot afloat on a beautiful but brutish river.

Chapter 3: A New World

They hiked along the perimeter of the floodwall, brushing against the late summer weeds, waist-high in some places, but also through open areas along the riverbank that had been picked clean of trash by the prisoners. Finally, Dale broke the silence. "Can't believe what we saw back there, Rodney. What do you suppose will become of those poor kids now that both their parents have been killed right there in front of them?"

Rodney stopped to remove some briars from his pant legs, then answered. "Either their shanty will get snagged in the willows along the big island or, more likely, it'll make it to the locks and dam below the island, probably in about another hour or so, maybe a little less. The river is high and running fast today, thanks to all the thunderstorms we've had lately, so the current will probably sweep them right by the island. At least, I hope it will. And once the shanty reaches the locks and dam, the Lockmaster will have to rescue the kids. Hopefully, that's what will happen. Otherwise, if they should get snagged in the willows along the island, it might be days before anyone even finds them. Either way, it's a terrible experience for anyone, let alone kids that young."

As they resumed walking, Dale said, "Just imagine how frightened those little kids must be right now!"

"That's for sure! Would scare the hell out of me, I know that!"

"Think we should tell somebody about them, Rodney—you know, just to make sure they do get rescued?"

"No, definitely not! We can't, because if we did, then we'd have to explain how we came to know about them, and that would lead to problems for us. I'd say the people in the remaining shantyboats are likely to be in trouble. Don't think it would shorten the rescue of the children much if we did report what happened to them, not as slow as things take place these days. Crime has become so routine that no one seems to care, except the victims themselves. Everybody else has become numb to the violence and robbery. Plus, even if someone does report what happened, the Federation will twist the case around to say that some good citizen—namely, the guard—killed the parents because they were abusing their kids. Why, just look how scary the community shelters can be. You never know if somebody is going to stiff you in the middle of the night, just because the soles of your shoes don't have holes in them yet the way his do. And when that happens, nothing is done about it. Just another dead vagrant to dispose of when the lights come on in the morning. That seems to be the Federation's view of it.

"All part of the cult of the underdog, Dale. One of the most insidious concepts in history but fundamental to the socialist world view we're living under today. Been going on for so long that the criminals think they are the righteous ones, because that's what the Federation has told them over and over again. So, now they think they're entitled to steal anything they can lay their hands on, even if they have to kill someone to do it. So, if we did report what we saw to any of the Federation officials, tell them that we personally saw one of their guards kill two innocent people and deliberately jeopardize the lives of two small children, we'd certainly be the ones to get into trouble. So, no, the best thing that can happen to those kids is that their shanty makes it to the locks as fast as possible without any report from us. Their runaway shanty will interfere with commercial traffic at the locks, and then something will have to be done. Otherwise, seems like the whole country has been turned into a pack of feral dogs, yelping and snapping and biting at one another, each trying to take advantage of the other. There's no expectation of one person helping another, even when children are involved."

"I understand what you're saying about underdogs, but those people in the shantyboats, aren't they underdogs, too? Sure as hell the guard wasn't."

"Anybody who resists the Federation, even over such a little thing as picking up trash, loses any favorable status he or she might have had as an underdog, regardless of looks or race or sex or economic condition or anything else. And loses it just that damn quick, too. Devotion to the Federation, which has become the same as devotion to the Parity Party, is all that counts.

"Besides, I expect the Federation doesn't much like either the shantyboats or the people on them, trash or no trash. The shanty folks are trying to live outside the system, beyond the Federation's control, trying for something the Federation absolutely fears— personal freedom. Because once people taste freedom, they want more of it. That means, from the Federation's point of view, they're subversives, not underdogs. So, it's all right for a guard to shoot them and for the Federation itself to pen them up like cattle and in

14

that way slowly kill them. No individual freedoms are allowed any more, not for shanty folks and not for anyone else. You owe your gratitude and your complete allegiance to the Federation alone, which, as I said, has become one and the same thing as the Parity Party.

"Think about it. It's the Federation that provides you with your livelihood through its canteens and shelters, even if those are paid for with money the Federation stole from you and me and everyone else who had even small amounts of money left after the Greater Depression started. First, they stole our money as taxes and later as outright banking account confiscations. Freeze your account first over some alleged crime and then drain it—that's their procedure. And their theft of all we worked for is what has caused us, directly or indirectly, to become homeless. They steal our money and then just print up new money when they run out of our money to steal. And that unrestricted printing makes worthless any money you might still have, whether it's in a bank or under your mattress or in your sock. Either way, through confiscation or inflation, we lose our money. You can't expect anything else, Dale. Not any more. Justice and the simplest case of private ownership, let alone the prosperity the country once knew, none of that is allowed, none of that is possible."

"But back to the kids, suppose the Lockmaster does rescue them, what then? What do you think he'll do with them?"

"He'll have them sent back up here to town, and the social services people will put them in one of the women and children's shelters for a while to get them evaluated. While they're there, shelter workers will be assigned to take care of them but instead will farm them out to one of the mothers using the shelter in exchange for extra food and clothing. When the kids' lives have settled down a bit, they'll probably be shipped off to one of the kids' camps, where they'll end up doing light labor in one of the factories, maybe stay there for the rest of their lives since they have no other family. That's the way things seem to be going. But who knows for sure?"

"Won't something good have to happen sooner or later, Rodney, to those kids, to us, to anybody?"

"Not if other parts of the world are examples. When did something good ever happen to the people in North Korea? Or in China? Or in the old Soviet Union, except for its ending? Even when

15

good does come along, as it did for that short while in Russia after the Soviet Union, it doesn't last. It's gone in a flash because the powerful can't tolerate even the simplest freedoms for the rest of us. They believe they know better than we do what's good for us. But what they really mean is what's good for them to get and keep power.

"Just imagine it this way, Dale. The Federation is like a huge python slithering out of the Everglades and coming up from the Florida peninsula into the rest of the country. Wherever it goes and whatever it sees that it wants, the python just throws its coils around that thing—our schools, our libraries, our courts, our businesses, even our children—and it constricts them until they conform to its shape and no longer have a shape of their own. That, I believe, is what has happened to us since the old 1789 Constitution was replaced by this new one. After that happened, there were no longer any powers left to the states and so, no force strong enough to stop the Federalist python. 'Federation' is just an empty word now in our country, a euphemism, really, for 'totalitarian,' not for shared power between the states and the national government.

"Just think of how our children, both yours and mine, have been lost to us. The python fastened itself onto them and their mothers, our wives, and carried them away into the underbrush, to places we can't even find. We might try to tell ourselves the loss is just temporary and that we'll get our families back, but by now we know we won't. It's like taking a deep breath to revive ourselves as we work, but when we do, the python, which knows everything we do before we do it, wraps itself even tighter around us. We can exhale but never inhale again. The python tightens and tightens until we can't breathe at all and die."

"Maybe you're right. Seems like all these camps they got for everybody these days are like those snake coils, doesn't it? Education camps to bring you into line and keep you there. Labor camps that work you to death if you go against the Federation. Kids camps with factory work if you got no family. Factory camps if you broke some other kind of law or some snitch says you did. Nobody just sits in jail any more, that's for sure. Got to work for the Federation or the companies the Federation sponsors to pay for your room and board in life, if you can really call it that."

"Yes," Rodney said, nodding his head, "you got it right. And that's exactly how we've brought manufacturing back to America, as the Federation likes to boast, by making available to the Federation-controlled industries the slave labor of prisoners. Companies that were too honorable to go along with that practice were run out of business. Yet—and it seems like a long time ago now—it was the Parity Party that was the big supporter of the labor unions. 'Workers of the world unite! You have nothing to lose but your chains!' Remember all that?"

"Not really, but wasn't that the communist slogan?"

"You bet it was, right from Marx and Engels in their *Communist Manifesto*. Well, all those sentiments are gone now, killed by the very people who screamed them the loudest and took to the streets to make them come true, yet now not a single prayer is said by any of them over the graves of the dead union leaders and won't be any time soon. Just one of the inevitable phases of history leading to the dictatorship we have now. The Parity Party is all about making new chains, not breaking old ones. They saw they could get more votes by going after minority group votes—that cult of the underdog again. Cobble enough of those together and you have a majority, and you win. So, that was the end of catering to the workers and their unions."

"That's for certain. I can hardly remember unions at all. Last ones disappeared when I was still a kid, I believe."

"Now, instead of helping unions, the Federation has to make sure there are enough prisoners to staff its sponsored factories, just like many other countries do. China, for example. Countries we used to look down on and accused of human rights violations. Don't hear that phrase any more, not since we're guilty of it ourselves. Plus, since we're all minorities now and the Federation has total control, it doesn't matter what racial or ethnic groups the prisoners come from as long as there's enough of them. As it turns out, affirmative action was just another path to political power. I notice it's not applied in deciding who goes to the labor camps."

"How did you get to know all these things, Rodney? Did you go to college?"

"I did, but only for two years. After that I got disillusioned with it, quit, and joined the Navy. Thought I would learn more there, since the colleges had become nothing more than propaganda

17

centers. I wanted a more practical education than I was getting. What I didn't count on was that the Federation had also ruined our Armed Forces. But the college exposure did cause me to pay more attention to what was going on with the government and to start worrying about the country's future. So, I took up studying those problems on my own."

"Well, what do you think will happen to that guard, then? Anything at all?"

"Not a single thing, Dale, unless it's a promotion. That would be my guess. The floodwall hid his murders from anyone in town, except us, and we don't dare tell anyone. As for the other guards, they certainly aren't going to squeal on their coworker. The other shantyboat people can't say anything that would be believed. Plus, you can bet they won't even dare to tell anyone for fear of losing what little freedom they have. The same reason you and I won't tell anyone, even though we want to help those poor frightened little kids. That only leaves the prisoners, and they, just like us, have no one to tell. If they tried, they'd be killed."

"Well, I still have a hankering to try out shantyboat life, despite what we just saw, if only to get that little taste of freedom you talked about. A lot less risky in a shanty than waking up in the middle of the night to some stranger pawing at you in one of these damn shelters and having to go and bust the guy's nose just to get him to stop. Then you have to deal with the shelter guards, who should have been the ones looking out for us as we slept but don't really care. They're usually off somewhere playing cards or watching old movies on a little TV. Or you're out in the streets and someone tries to cut your throat for a pair of shoes 'cause yours got more leather than his do and there's nobody to help you. Damn, Rodney, what do you think? Should we try it? Try to build a shanty?"

"I'm willing if you are, Dale. Won't be easy but worth the effort, I think. We'll need a lot of material, though. Not sure how we'll come up with that, but the people in the shanties we just saw did it."

"Since you're interested in building a shantyboat, too, I'm glad we've come up this direction. It's not only shorter to reach the end of the floodwall this way, but just across that bridge over there is a canteen and a shelter—over there in Southside. You familiar with that side of town?"

18

"No, can't say that I know all that much about Southside. Never went there much."

"I know it really well," Dale declared. "Grew up there. Hell, we kids used to play ball within sight of where the shelter and canteen are now, played in a ballfield in the flats down by the river. And not far upriver from the canteen is the lumberyard where I used to work. About a mile walk, I'd say, maybe not that much. After lunch we could hike up there and see what's left to work with. Who knows, might be enough left there to build a shantyboat. When I got laid off, there was still a lot of lumber and other materials there that we couldn't sell any more 'cause the Federation didn't want more trees to be cut down. Bad for the environment, they said, but apparently just fine for forest fires. Anway, since you couldn't build anything new from wood, a person could only repair what was old. Still that way. So, soon enough that was the end of the building contractors, and without them for customers, that was soon the end of the lumberyard and our jobs along with it.

"And now, since there is no longer any new wood coming to market, the price of lumber has shot up tremendously. But do you really think we can even get into the yard to find out what's there? Probably locked up tight by now; otherwise, everything would be stolen."

"Well, if they haven't switched out the locks, I got a key," Dale announced proudly. "Kept it when I left. Been transferring it from one set of clothes to the next when I change old for new in the shelters. Guess nobody knew I had it or just forgot I did. Leastways they never asked me for it, and I've held onto it ever since, though I'd just about lost hope of ever using it for anything. There's a back gate to the fence that runs round the yard. Back gate's on the river side, and that lock works off this same key." By now, Dale had fished the key from a pocket and held it up for Rodney to see. "At least, it used to work. So, if we come and go that back way, there's less chance anybody from the street would see us."

"Well then, let's go check it out," Rodney said as he started up the bank to the bridge deck. "Seems like it can't do any harm to look."

"Okay," Dale replied, "but first let's stop at the canteen on the other side of the bridge here 'cause it might close before we finish at the yard. Besides, I'm hungry as hell. How 'bout you?"

19

Chapter 4: Food

The Southside Community Canteen #2 had once been an auto dealership, but since individual ownership of vehicles was no longer permitted except for business purposes, allegedly to protect the environment but more likely to improve Federalist control over travel, the dealership owner had been forced to close his businesses, laying off fifteen employees at the time, and thereby adding another trickle to the flood of the unemployed. Trucks, mostly used ones, could still be purchased or rented for commercial use, but even those sales were closely regulated by the Federation. Consequently, nearly everyone was now forced onto public conveyances for local transportation, usually buses or vans. Single use permits were needed for long distance travel by air or bus, and those were difficult to obtain for most people.

Inside the canteen, the lunch queue was already more than thirty vagrants long when Dale and Rodney arrived. Immediately inside the entrance, a security guard was wanding each vagrant who entered with a metal detector, searching for possible weapons, while another guard scanned each vagrant's microchip. All vagrants, in order to receive Federation services, had to wear a tiny microchip fastened behind their right earlobe. Scanning the microchips at the canteens and shelters provided a record of the services each vagrant received and at which facility. It also helped authorities identify the corpses found so often in the streets and alleys, along the riverbanks, and sometimes deep in the woodlands. Thugs and thieves, however, had for their part learned to snip off the earlobes, if not cut off the entire ear, before leaving their victims and disposing of the earlobe in another location. As for Rodney, he had learned long ago to hide his knife outdoors before entering the canteens and shelters and retrieve it later; otherwise, it would have been confiscated.

As the line inside the canteen grew, it eventually snaked around the room's perimeter, encircling its long rows of rough but sturdy picnic-style tables with attached benches, jammed end to end. Tissue-thin white vinyl tablecloths, often still soiled and stained with use, covered the tables. Eventually, the queue led to the serving tables. There, awaiting the vagrants, were stacks of red plastic trays, white plastic bowls, and black plastic utensils. Unbroken utensils had been retrieved from the breakfast trash, then hastily washed and returned to use, often with flecks of food still stuck to them. Beside the utensils stood rolls of paper towels to be used as napkins. Then came cauldrons of thin cabbage soup dispensed by the indifferent canteen staff using long-handled ladles. Next to the cauldrons were stacks of bread slices, hastily buttered, and more often than not stale. Next came trays of plastic cups filled with a pale yellow mystery juice. And finally, there were columns of brown paper cups for the weak coffee that could be self-dispensed from a row of multi-gallon metal urns.

Occasionally the canteen soup was fortified with bits of meat, usually fatty ham or grisly beef transformed by a long boil into a gelatinous mass. But not today. Today's soup consisted of the usual watery pale green cabbage and a few mushy carrot medallions, the latter added both for a dash of color and an unenthusiastic attempt at nutrition. On holidays the meat was more plentiful, the soup a bit thicker, the coffee a tad stronger, and the stale bread replaced with diagonally cut honey sandwiches or cornbread.

At Christmas there were even sweet rolls. Odd, in that celebrations of the Nativity were not permitted any longer. The Federation had discarded Christmas as part of a harmful superstition that was especially offensive to many of the government's supporters. In fact, the government had jettisoned all Christian theology as misinformation that was dangerous for the Federation's citizens. Consequently, some of the larger, more substantial churches had been turned into community shelters, since these were in great demand. Smaller, flimsier ones were simply demolished or converted into low rent apartments. Despite the Federation's efforts at extinguishing religious faith, rumors of secret congregations abounded, some of these congregations even claiming to have maintained Apostolic Succession and offering the Divine Eucharist.

With their trays finally supplied with soup, bread, and drinks, Dale and Rodney sought out an isolated spot where they could talk over their shantyboat idea without interruption or the threat of eavesdropping. For many eager ears were waiting to capture incriminating conversations that could be sold to the Federation. Everyone knew that informers were rewarded with nearly new clothes and a fine meal that included a choice of beer or wine served in a private room just behind the city workers' cafeteria in the city building. Just one such meal was allowed per informer and only when the informer's information produced a new prisoner or two. But by now many also knew that informers rarely lived to enjoy a second meal, even in the canteens. Instead, their corpses were found tossed over embankments, stripped of their new clothes, their new shoes, their old lives, and their right earlobes. Still, many took the risk of informing, hoping for the joys of an enduring anonymity after a good meal, even if that meant bartering away the new clothes to make themselves less conspicuous.

Sitting opposite each other in an open area at the end of one row of benches, Dale and Rodney began their discussion. "Well, as I was saying before, do you suppose we could throw in together and get some advantage from it?" Dale asked as he stirred his soup with a plastic spoon he hoped was new. "What do you think?"

Rodney sipped some of his soup while listening to Dale, paused a moment, considering Dale's proposal, and then asked, "You still mean to build a shantyboat, then, and share it? Is that what you're saying?"

"That's it," Dale said as he looked to his right and then his left. "Too hard a project for one fellow to take on by himself, but together two guys could pull it off before cold weather sets in this fall. It's plenty hot today, but the first frost will be here before you know it. What do you think, Rodney? Should we try it? Looks like a lot of other people have managed it."

Pausing to test a spoonful of his own soup, Rodney finally nodded his head and replied, "Believe we could. Yes, I think the two of us could do it before winter. And should do it. Of course, everything depends on finding the right materials and the right hardware to go with it. That's the key to the whole thing. And we'd at least want to make it more comfortable than the community shelters. Otherwise, there's no point in doing it other than gaining some privacy."

Then Dale took up the shanty cause again. "Also, it would give us our own place to go in the winter instead of having to try to get into a shelter only to find it full already. Might even have to defend our shantyboat on those cold winter days just to keep it ours. Even in good weather, it would be a place to rest instead of just trudging around the streets all the time. And what with your experience in junk yards and mine in lumberyards and carpentry in general, we just might come up with what we need in supplies and know-how. I worked as a privately employed handyman doing odds and ends of household repairs for people before getting my job in the lumberyard. Don't believe my old place is being worked any more. Doubt if yours is, either. My guess is they're both just being raided as people need to make repairs, since they can't get help any more to fix anything and can't buy anything new that's worth having from these damn prison factories the Federation sponsors, even if they had the money to do it. That stuff is as bad as the junk we used to get from China." Dale had bent his head toward Rodney and was whispering this part. "So, people got to do for themselves these days as best they can. That's the way I see it."

"You realize we'll need tools as well as materials. I forgot to mention those—saws and hammers, and at least two hand drills of some kind, with drill bits. And I'm sure a lot of other things we won't think of until we need them. Going to be slow work without power tools."

"Right you are again. I've not forgotten about the tools. Saws and hammers, plus fasteners of one kind and another, need all of them. Maybe we need a hardware man to join us. Somebody who knows even better than we do where to find hardware, tools, and the like."

"No, no, can't get too big. The more people involved, the greater the risk of being found out. Besides, a shantyboat such as we'll be lucky to build won't accommodate three. In fact, it'll do well to serve the two of us comfortably. And one more person just increases the chances of a snitch."

"Okay, reckon you're right again. You have something in mind then about the size and look of a shanty, or would you just be willing to go for something like the ones we saw today down on the river?"

"I think all those shanties we saw moored down by the old park were a bit too narrow and top-heavy. Also, their weight is not distributed properly. That makes them ride too low in the water. Probably built in haste and without much skill or knowledge of boat building. In a bad storm the people in those shanties could find themselves in trouble plenty quick, especially if the wind got high and the water choppy. Their shanties would take on water. I'm not saying they would capsize—they probably are too wide for that— but they would take on water, maybe even get swamped and sink.

After all, shanties are flat-bottomed boats with no keels and no ballast to keep them stable in the water."

"Wow, you sound just like a sailor, Rodney! Keels and ballast, my word! I would never have thought of those things."

"As I said, I was a sailor. US Navy for five years, back when the country still had a navy, that is. Before the new constitution made us the Federated States of America. But Mighty America is no more, as we all know."

"As misfortune has it, you're right again. I remember the Happy Times, just barely, though. I heard we were always worried back then about getting invaded by the Russians or the Chinese or such and the like. Leastways, that's what I was told. But we had a good army and navy in those days and an air force, too, I hear."

"We did, but we've got nothing now except the Federation Police everywhere you turn, one police force for the whole country. No one realized back then that the biggest enemy was right here all along, right inside our own borders, inside our own government, not somewhere overseas. Now we citizens get treated like we're the ones who are the enemy."

"I'd sure join up this very day if we still had an army. If nothing else, it'd beat the hell out of not knowing if you'll get to eat today and where you'll sleep tonight."

"Yes, but you don't have that option any more. No one does, at least not voluntarily. And the country's enemies have no need to invade us now. We've already done ourselves in, as they very well know. Just look at us—spent ourselves flat broke as a country, and now we just sit here, once proud Americans, with our butts on government canteen benches trying to think of a way to build a pitiful little shantyboat just so we can have a little bit of privacy and shelter of our own—and even that not on dry land! And with no hope of ever having a house and family of our own again, either. This isn't America any more, Dale. I don't know what it is. Call it the Federated States of America if you like, but it's not America, not the United States we knew when we were young."

"Seems like a crime, doesn't it? How all that happened. And happened so fast you'd almost think somebody planned it that way." Dale stopped and gave Rodney a close look. "Say, you must be a bit older than I am, aren't you?"

"Well, I'm forty-two, Dale."

"And I'm thirty-two."

"Just as I was saying, after a long, slow decline, the collapse came very fast—the Big Collapse leading to the Greater Depression we're in now. All told, the Great Collapse took just five years once it really got rolling with businesses and banks failing all over the country and the Federation then taking control of them. But it had been brewing politically and socially for a lot longer. Decades longer. Back as far as the Viet Nam War I've heard some older people say, so nearly a hundred years of gradual decline. But at the end, things happened fast, the way water speeds up going down a drain."

"Whew, Viet Nam! Now, that is a long way back there!"

"Yes, but by the time I was in the Navy, my service only made good training for working in a junk yard, because that's all we had left to work with and sail in—junk. We couldn't have won a war if the enemy had given us a five-year warning and let us shoot first."

"Really? I just don't know as much about all that's happened to us as I should. Too young, I guess. Too stupid to boot, I suppose. Got no real learning from school. Teachers didn't seem to know anything themselves about what they were supposed to be teaching—the math, science, history, and so forth. Just knew what the government told them to teach, and that was nothing you could really use in life, nothing practical. Just what the Feds wanted you to believe so's to make you go along with what they wanted, I guess. Least that's the way it seemed to me."

"Well, no point in trying to relive it all now," Rodney said. "This is where we are."

"Right you are again. Now, back to this swamping and sinking problem with the shanties. How would you propose to solve those, Mr. Navy Man?"

"Pontoons would be ideal. If you can't have a keel and ballast, you need to distribute the weight of the craft over a broad area, port to starboard and bow to stern, yet have the deck high enough above the water to avoid swamping. Across a set of pontoons secured below a wide deck would be the ideal design. Not only keeps the deck well above the water but still makes the boat stable in choppy waters. Need three pontoons the length of the deck or a bit longer if you can get them, one on each side and one down the middle, but two would work fine for the size boat we'll need. We're not going to sea in a shantyboat, after all. Hopefully, never even have to move the shanty. Besides, we'd be lucky to find or make two pontoons let alone three. And what's more, they'll need to be identical or else the shanty would be lopsided and no fun to live on."

"Well, I understand now what you're saying, and I agree about the pontoons. They won't be easy to find, not at all."

"No, but we might find barrels. Watertight barrels could be made to do the trick. and if we could find plastic ones big enough, they'd last a long time instead of rusting out underneath us the way metal ones would do."

"Really! Well now, I do know where we just might find those. If they're still there, that is."

"Where's that?"

"At the lumberyard, again, the one I was telling you about—just up the street a bit. The yard's been abandoned now and locked up for months, but we might be able to get most of what we need there, at least I believe so. And we used to have plastic barrels with lids. Sold wooden stakes and dowels and such in them. Suppose they could be made watertight if we were careful about it. Plus, we sold wood screws and nails—all the fasteners you could ever need, if they're still there."

"And the junkyard where I worked probably still has a lot of hardware of many different kinds lying around, if it's not all been stolen. Likely some old tools, as well. We used a wide variety of hand tools to take parts off junked items to sell separately."

"So, barrels for pontoons, huh? Now I can see how those would work." Dale stirred the remainder of his soup thoughtfully. As he dipped the last bit of his bread into it, he said, "One thing for sure I have learned from all I've lost this last little while—having someone to talk to, just that alone, is worth a fortune. If you put a pile of gold coins in front of me right now, I'd turn them down for companionship. Just someone to share your troubles with, so's you know you're not alone in this world, bad as it's become. Besides, you can't buy anything worth having any more, not even with gold coins."

Rodney, who was tilting his empty soup bowl back and forth on the table absentmindedly while warily studying the other vagrants near them, now looked Dale in the eyes, rubbed his whiskered chin thoughtfully and smiled, before declaring, "This time, Dale, you're the one who's right. You just spoke the most truthful words of all we've said between us so far. Thanks."

Chapter 5: Lumberyard

So, the two resolved to build a shantyboat. Dale's key did, indeed, unlock the gate at the rear of the lumberyard, which sat about fifty feet above the river. They entered the yard and climbed a small embankment up to the storage sheds near the street, avoiding the open area of the driveway that ran from the front gate to the rear one. The sheds were large, each one being about two stories high and sixty feet long, three of them in a long row, the first two separated from the third by the yard's entrance drive and office building, all strung out along Camden Avenue, one of the main streets in Southside. Once inside the first shed, they found it still surprisingly well-stocked.

"Hell, a fellow could get by in one of these sheds, during warm weather, leastways," Dale said as he looked around the interior, surveying the building materials. "Toss one of those padded sleeping bags up on a stack of these plywood panels and you could lay up in there and sleep pretty well, I'd think. Surprised nobody's doing it."

"True, but that probably means the place gets inspected every so often," Rodney cautioned. "And who would want to climb that fence every day just to come and go? That's why there's still lumber here, too. The possibility of a guard inspecting the place is something we'll need to consider as we 'borrow' supplies. Wonder if someone has a good inventory record of what's here?"

"Oh, I'm sure ole man Badgett does, if he's still around. Walter Badgett, he's the one who owns this place, and he was always careful about keeping track of every dime coming in or going out and every second of time we all worked or didn't. He wouldn't even let us leave the premises for lunchtime. Couldn't even visit the diner just up the street. Had to bring our lunches and eat them inside these storage sheds—hot weather or cold. But the old bastard mostly kept things like inventories to himself, so I doubt if a lowly security guard would know the inventory counts. He'd have to go by the looks of things from one inspection to the next to know if something might be missing."

"Well, let's hope so. And hope, too, that the guard, if there is one, isn't very observant."

"Just look at all the lumber that's still here. Two-by-fours and two-by-sixes in these racks right here beside us!" Dale placed his hand on one of the two-by-sixes, giving it an affectionate pat. "Way more than enough for us to use. And plywood panels over there on the other side of the shed. All just waiting for the good ole days to return and contractors to start putting up homes and office buildings again, ones made out of lumber. This is much more than I expected to find, it really is. What do you think, Rodney?"

"Well, let's look around some more. What about fasteners? Didn't you say the yard sold those, too—nails and screws and bolts?"

"Sure did. All kinds and all sizes. Nails and wood screws mostly. Nearly as good a business for us as the lumber. Sold some bolts, nuts, and washers, too, but not so many of those. Kept all that kind of stuff in the main building where the offices and the cashier were located. Little stuff like that was too easy to steal from the sheds. But no tools to speak of, except for a few saws and the tools we workers used. Kept those in the little workshop inside the third storage shed."

"And what about the blue barrels you mentioned—where are they?"

"Oh, yeah, should be in the third shed, also, on the other side of the entrance, right beyond the office building. Come on over this way and we'll take a look." Dale pointed out the direction as he walked out of the shed.

He started across the yard's entrance drive but kept looking across the street as he walked. Then in the middle of the drive, he stopped suddenly and extended his arms like a crossing guard to stop Rodney, as well. "Damnation!" he said. "Let's get back inside the shed!"

They hustled back to the second shed. There Dale, peeking out of the doorway said, "Thought I saw someone across the street, in that first house there." He pointed to a small white two-story house that sat diagonally across the street from the lumberyard's entrance gate. "Thought I saw someone in that upstairs window just now. My supervisor, Randy Hodge—well, the guy who used to be my supervisor leastways—he lived over there. Maybe still does for all I know. He and his wife, Delia, and their little boy, Sammy. Last time I spoke with him, the day we all got laid off, said he thought he'd go

29

on up toward Pittsburgh to find work. Much bigger town, so more opportunities; that was his thinking. Said he'd been considering it for a while."

Rodney could hear in Dale's voice and see in his eyes a curious combination of dread and hope. "Well, was it his face you saw, this supervisor? You think he's still around? Would mean bad trouble for us if he sees us in here and calls the Federation police."

"No, don't think it was him. Looked more like a woman, so probably Delia just looking out the window. Happened so quick I can't be sure. Didn't get a good look before whoever it was pulled the blind down. And that wouldn't be like him anyway. Maybe her but not him. He'd be over here right now wanting to know what's going on. Another thing to keep an eye on, though. Feels like we're getting into something dangerous here, doesn't it?"

"Does that mean you want to stop now before we get too far into this project to get out?"

"No. No, not at all. I'm all for building us a boat, I really am. We'll just have to keep an eye on that place, that's all I'm saying. Even if he is there, I can talk to him, him or Delia, either one. Convince them not to report us. Don't think they would anyway. Besides, seeing someone over here might even make them happy. Start them to thinking the yard's going to open again. Come on, let's go on and check out the next shed and office building."

They made it across the entrance drive this time without further incident and walked behind the office building before entering the next shed where they did, indeed, find an inventory of blue plastic barrels, all but three of them still containing stakes and large diameter dowels.

Rodney rolled one of the empty barrels over to the shed entrance to examine it better in the sunlight. "I believe these will work, Dale. They've got flanges both top and bottom where brackets can grab hold. Got lids and straight sides. No bungs to leak. Just need to seal the lids up tight and test them in the river. Then find brackets to attach them securely to the underside of the deck we'll build."

"Well, good. But we don't have the brackets you said we need."

"No, but I think we can get those at my junkyard. We used to separate hardware and parts from junked items if we thought we could sell them separately. That actually kept us busier than helping customers and made money faster, too. We had a wide variety of tools there that we used to remove parts, since we never knew what we'd get into, and most of them were manual tools, since we had to do most of the work out in the yard without electricity. Those would be perfect for what we'll need to use here, since there's no electricity available."

"But can we get into your junkyard? Do you have a key for it the way I do for this place?"

"No, the owner was careful to take mine when he laid me off, but I'll find a way in, don't worry about that. Security was never very good there. Just a Rottweiler on a long chain. A bigger problem will be transporting what we need back here if it's bulky. We may need a truck at some point, and that would draw attention."

"We'll just have to manage somehow. Let's try to get in the office building next to see what's in there."

Dale's key did not work in either of the office building's doors. He didn't think it would, but they found one of the rear sash windows that wasn't locked. They were able to push it up with a narrow stick and enter. Inside, they found nails of all types and sizes, wood screws, as well, plus bolts and nuts for various applications, just as Dale said. In fact, the entire lumberyard was just waiting to come to life again.

"Tell you what, Dale," Rodney said as he grabbed a pencil and writing pad from one of the office desks, "let's make a list of what we need that's not available here. Then we'll visit the junkyard tomorrow to see if we can find the rest. Might take more than one trip to haul what we need back over here, but at least we'll know if this project is doable. That okay with you?"

"Good, I'm all for it. Before we start, though, I want to look in ole man Badgett's office." Dale motioned toward a door in the corner of the main office. "Always wondered what it was like in there. Let's take a peek."

With little effort they managed to force the door open, defeating a rather simple interior lock without breaking anything. Inside the tiny office they found a desk still strewn with papers, pens and pencils, an old-fashioned adding machine, a calculator, and pictures of children posing with a dour-looking woman.

"Just like ole man Badgett, this office is," Dale chirped. "Yep, just like him. He'd stand here in the corner by these two windows so's he could keep watch on things. Look out one way to the street entrance gate and look the other way toward one side of the yard to make sure nobody was loafing. If they were, he'd come running out, raising a fuss like you never heard."

"Looks like he's been here recently," Rodney added, "judging by the condition of his desk. And look, his desk calendar's been turned to June 30th, only a few days ago. I believe today's July Fourth, so I'll bet the 30th is when he was here last, maybe doing some month-end calculations."

"You could be right. That would be just like him. That picture there of that nasty-looking woman and grandkids—that's his family. I know that much about him. They were all in here one day. He was giving the grandkids a tour of the place while his wife—Agnes is her name—just tagged along, looking out of place and angry. Seems like it was just the other day that happened."

Rodney gazed around the office as Dale recalled the Badgett family visit. He moved about with cautious steps in the crowded office until one object grabbed his attention.

"Dale, take a look at this." Rodney pointed to a small wood-burning stove set into an alcove behind the desk, vented through the side wall with stove pipe. It was a black iron cylinder about three feet tall with a bronzed conical cap decorated with scrolls and other flourishes of a blacksmith's artistry. Its small black fire door had a wire spring handle.

"Oh, yeah, the office clerks always said Badgett liked old antiquey things. He liked to think of himself as one of those early industry guys like Rockefeller or Carnegie from whatever period of time that was."

"You mean the Gilded Age—last decade of the nineteenth century?"

"I guess so—when we had industries starting up all over the country. You seem to know about those kinds of things better than I do. Anyways, he collected stuff from that period. This old adding machine here on his desk—he called it a comptometer or something like that. Anyhow, that's one example of his nostalgia, and I guess that little stove is another. He even liked to dress himself in that old style, too. Kept time with an old pocket watch on a gold chain. He was always pulling it out of its little pocket in his vest or along the belt line of his trousers to check the time. Who the hell even wears

32

a vest these days, I'd like to know. Anyhow, he'd pull out that pocket watch by a gold chain with a gold coin fob attached. He'd check the time and make quite a show of it, even though he also wore a wristwatch. We used to joke that the pocket watch was probably really a stopwatch so's he could check how fast we were working. That's just the kind of guy he was. And I'd guess, judging by this desk here, still is. He did have a cell phone, though. Called it his pocket phone."

"Well, that little stove and its vent pipe are exactly what we'll need to heat the shanty's cabin when we've got it built. We'll need to remember that."

"By golly, you're right. Hadn't thought that far ahead yet. We'll just borrow it from him when the time comes."

"And while we have pencil and paper handy here, I'll make a sketch or two with some rough dimensions to help guide us along the way in building the shantyboat."

"Sounds good. You might just as well sit down at ole man Badgett's desk and help yourself to his supplies. He probably even has a T-square and drawing board around here somewhere."

"Well, at your invitation, I believe I'll just do that," Rodney replied, laughing. "I think a simple sketch or two will do, however, so no need for the T-square. We're not going to build an aircraft carrier, after all."

Thanks to training in drafting, Rodney soon had three reasonably proportional drawings of the shantyboat he had in mind—two exterior views and the interior of a cabin. The boat deck consisted of one-by-six-inch planks screwed to a frame of two-by-sixes, to which in turn were fastened the six plastic barrels, three equally spaced under each side of the deck. As Rodney completed a section of each drawing, he would call out the materials, fasteners, and tools they would need, plus their sizes and quantities. As he did, Dale collected this information on a bill of materials he had started on a separate sheet of paper. Hammers, saws, drills and drill bits, screwdrivers of various types, hinges, a door, windows, and the precious brackets. The more they envisioned the shanty, the longer the list grew and the more their desire to get started swelled.

When they finally looked up from their work, they saw the lengthening shadows outside the office and decided that it was time to make their way to the nearest shelter for the night.

"If we don't hustle," Dale cautioned, "we won't make the shelter's seven o'clock curfew. Then we will find out what it's like to sleep in one of these storage sheds!"

Chapter 6: Shelter

Located next to its corresponding community canteen, the same one where Dale and Rodney had eaten lunch, stood the Southside Community Men's Shelter #2, a building of fabricated steel much newer than its converted auto dealership neighbor that housed the Southside Community Men's Canteen #2. The nearest shelter and canteen for women and children was more than a mile away, meaning that vagrant families were separated for meals and shelter unless they could make do for themselves.

The Southside Shelter #2, a newer fabricated steel building, consisted of a large rectangular sleeping area on the main floor accommodating 120 narrow cots arranged, barracks style, in a grid of long rows and columns evenly divided by a center aisle. The position of each cot was designated by four small yellow circles painted on the smooth grey concrete floor.

Most of the vagrants chose to sleep in their clothes and use one of their blankets as a pillow, since there were never enough pillows for everyone. In cold weather the building was adequately heated to sixty-five degrees. In the summer cross ventilation and large overhead fans cooled the area to a bearable temperature, typically around seventy-five degrees, but otherwise there was no air conditioning.

To the left of the entrance was a set of metal stairs leading to a mezzanine overlooking the sleeping area, and on that mezzanine were the offices of the shelter's staff. The mostly bare wall on the far side of the building opposite the offices displayed a large TV screen. All the beds were positioned so that the vagrants could watch the screen, as the Federation news was broadcast for their benefit from 7:00 to 8:00 PM each day. The news was followed by an entertainment film, which, like the news, was filled with political messaging intended to promote conformance to Federation policies. So far, there were only thirty of these films in circulation, shown each night in a revolving schedule throughout the country, month after month. More films were promised but so far not produced, their creation apparently awaiting new issues the Federation officials believed might require either dampening down or amping up. When the day's film ended at 9:00 PM, the shelter's lights dimmed and after ten minutes more shut off, leaving only some perimeter and

35

aisleway night lights plus any office lights that still happened to be in use shining from the mezzanine, usually only that of the shelter's night manager.

Beneath the mezzanine was a first aid clinic and a small infirmary that accommodated four beds, a small version of the much larger infirmaries that were part of the women and children's shelters. Also, one of the offices on the mezzanine was used by the doctors who rotated among the town's shelters during the day, a place away from the hubbub of the infirmary where they could retreat to record their notes and enter case data into the National Universal Medical Database. Most of the treatments and therapies, however, were administered and recorded by nurses or nurses' aides, especially during the evening hours, since the licensed physicians had become so few in number that they were in constant demand. After 9:00 PM medical services were only provided to vagrants on a call-in basis.

Despite the medical care being offered at no cost to the patients, everyone complained about its quality. Treatments for the vagrants was especially haphazard. The youngest and least capable doctors and nurses served in the community shelters. Successful treatments there, and to some degree everywhere, had become a matter more of chance than medical science, since the Parity Party had petitioned the Federation to abolish professional testing requirements nationwide both for entrance to medical schools and for graduation from them. And whatever the Parity Party wanted eventually found its way into practice, whether by legislation or executive order.

Testing was discriminatory, the Party claimed, a violation of human rights and a barrier to disadvantaged peoples, meaning anyone who lacked the skill and ability to become a medical professional but nevertheless could be verified as a Party supporter. The Parity Party's sole opponent, the Liberty Party, made several feeble attempts to prevent the proposal from becoming law, but as usually happened, whatever the Parity Party wanted, the Federation agreed to provide after a brief pretense of deliberation, for the Freedom Party, best known for its ineptitude, served as little more than a perennial strawman for the Paritions to thrash in each election. Most people had come to believe that the Freedomist politicians were paid to play their losing roles, like the no-name opponents in the phony drama of professional wrestling, and didn't in any case have the abilities required to serve the Federation responsibly.

After the no-testing policy was adopted and enforced nationwide, the quality of medical care began an uninterrupted decline and produced no appreciable increase in medical professionals. Similar effects followed in other professions and skilled trades that had previously relied on testing and apprenticeship programs to enforce quality standards and codes of professional conduct. These occupations were also gradually brought under the new law's umbrella with the net effect of steadily declining quality in services of all kinds in all regions of the country, thus adding greatly to the nation's general misery. But since the country's democracy had devolved for all practical purposes into one-party rule, the ballot box offered no corrective recourse.

At the rear of the shelter was the service area. In the far right corner was the Community Closet, more familiarly known among the vagrants as the "Rag Room." There the vagrants could exchange their worn and soiled clothing for freshly laundered clothes. These clean clothes were folded, though unsorted by size, and placed in large canvas laundry carts—one for shirts, another for pants. Freshly laundered grey tube socks, unisize, and grey underwear, also unsorted by size, were available from large cardboard shipping cartons set on folding tables along one wall. In wintry weather hooded coats, jackets, and sacks of unsized gloves and mittens were also made available and displayed on roll-about garment racks. Laundry carts positioned against another wall received the vagrants' discarded clothing. Against the Community Closet's back wall was a bank of plastic shelves displaying replacement shoes, both leather and canvas. These were, surprisingly, organized by size, though often unreliably. Vagrants placed their worn-out shoes in a large barrel at one side of the shelving once they had found reasonably suitable replacements. The staff sorted all the discards, both shoes and clothing, examining each item for the possibility of repair, laundering, and return to use.

Nowhere in the shelter were there fitting rooms. Vagrants had to exchange their clothes as best they could while standing on the concrete floor in full view of the shelter's staff and the other vagrants. And once a vagrant donned a garment, he could not, for reasons of hygiene and control, put it back. No matter how ill-fitting the garment was, he was stuck with it until at least the next day. Consequently, once a vagrant found something that fit him properly, he was reluctant to surrender it until its odor or condition became even more unbearable than the risk of surrendering it for an ill-fitting replacement. The failure to organize the clothing by size in any reliable manner seemed deliberate to the vagrants, an additional punishment to those who had fallen into the degradations of vagrancy.

Immediately adjacent to the Community Closet was a large laundry room. There the shelter's staff daily washed the blankets, towels, and exchanged clothing after inspecting them. Generally, anything without unrepairable rips and holes—whether clothing, blankets, or towels—was considered eligible for continued use or repair in accordance with the Federation mandate that all resources it provided had to be recycled until their utility was exhausted. This recycling policy meant that vagrants often dried themselves with towels so thin they no longer absorbed water sufficiently and wore garments that allowed the winter air to seep through them.

The largest portion of the shelter's service area was devoted to the shower room. The showers consisted of a long white fiberglass drainage basin with ten shower nozzles protruding from a white fiberglass wall. The showers were turned on when the first vagrants arrived each evening and were turned off at 9:00 PM, even if some vagrants were still waiting a turn. Sometimes, late arrivals would wallow desperately on the floor of the shower area, trying to clean themselves in the remaining water until it all drained. No individual temperature controls were provided. Below each nozzle was mounted a large dispenser of white liquid soap that served for both body wash and shampoo.

The shower area was completely open, with only a low step-over wall that served as a splash guard to keep the floor dry and to separate the shower area from the rest of the room. After their hasty showers, vagrants stepped into drying areas at either end of the bank of showers. Outside these areas, on tables along the low wall, were stacks of undyed cotton towels, located so that the vagrants could reach them. Attendants with mops and spray bottles of disinfectant circulated in the area in a largely vain effort to keep the floors dry and thereby reasonably safe. Slips, falls and injuries were, nevertheless, quite common. Canvas laundry carts stood by the drying areas to receive the vagrants' wet towels.

As for the toilets, there were ten of those, separated by partitions but without privacy doors. They lined the wall on either side of the shower room's entrance, five per side, opposite the showers. Throughout the evening, the toilets were constantly occupied while a queue of impatient vagrants waited their turn in queues snaking outside the shower room. The vagrant next in line for a toilet stood with his back to the current occupant and thus served as a privacy screen. Anyone failing to do this was quickly reminded to do so by the other vagrants.

In every respect both the shelters and the canteens were designed to reinforce the Federation's desired sense of community and parity while suppressing any expectation of personal privacy, personal property, or personal rights of any kind. In fact, such thoughts were officially regarded as selfish tendencies, which, if left unchecked, would undermine the foundations of the selfless behavior on which the Federation claimed it depended. Further, the Federation claimed that such thinking would inevitably lead to sedition. Consequently, the government worked diligently, through the Parity Party, to foster, implement, and when necessary enforce the nation's prime virtue, conformity.

In actuality, however, the conditions in the canteens and shelter provoked in the vagrants a sense of personal deprivation rather than the joyous shared sense of community depicted in the Federation's propaganda films. What the vagrants actually held in common was despair and a gradually developed code of conduct of their own, which required allowing for one another's privacy as much as possible and the murdering of Federation informers as quickly as possible.

When Dale and Rodney arrived at the shelter and offered their right ear lobes to the doorperson for scanning, it was almost 6:47 PM. Having spent so much time at the lumberyard, they had missed their chance for dinner in the Southside Community Canteen #2 next door, where vagrants were exiting and by now nearly filling the shelter. Once inside, most of the late arrivals went first to the Rag Room, then to the showers, and then to the sleeping area, where each tried to claim a cot in a favored location, usually in the darkest corners.

With just a few more arrivals after Dale and Rodney, the scanned data told the door monitor that bed capacity had been reached. The door monitor then informed the security guard standing nearby, and the security guard locked the entrance. This was often done, as it was on this night, in the faces of late arrivals, who would cry out, claiming they needed medical service. *At least let us see the doctor or a nurse!* But by that time the shelter door was firmly shut and locked for the night, so those cries were ignored, leaving the excluded outside to fend for themselves in the darkening streets and alleys and along the damp riverbanks. If they were alert enough and lucky enough, a few of them might find an abandoned building in which to spend the night, a benevolent turn of fate which they would try their best to conceal from their comrades of the streets, since the competition for abandoned buildings was keen, especially in the winter, and sometimes led to murders.

As for Dale and Rodney, this night they hustled through their showers and toilet turns. They had previously divided up the shantyboat documents they had prepared and concealed them in their exchanged clothing. Rodney kept the shanty drawings folded twice in his hip pocket, while Dale folded the bill of materials four times and placed it inside the one pocket of his fresh pants that was still sewn across the bottom. But trying to retain anything made undressing, the search for new clothes of the proper size, and redressing all the more difficult.

After finding the last open cots, the two watched, along with the other vagrants who were still awake, the large TV screen opposite them. It was showing the last scenes of a melodrama about the virtues of conformance, how cooperation at all levels produces a peaceful society and contented citizens, people willing to accept the loss of everything they have ever known, since these material goods, they now must realize, were acquired through selfish impulses and at the expense of their fellow citizens. In order to avoid future conflict and thus serve the greater good of all citizens in the Federation, they must comply with Federation policies, which had been adopted, after all, to create and maintain the greater good by an unnamed, an unknowable, and in effect an unelected elite. Then the lights above them, suspended from the shelter's steel girders, first dimmed and gradually darkened, ending another day in the purgatory of vagrancy and conformity.

40

Chapter 7: Scavenging

The next morning, Dale and Rodney wolfed down a canteen breakfast of oatmeal and raisins that seemed especially satisfying after their unplanned fast of the previous evening. Afterward, they boarded a bus headed for the north side of town.

During the bus ride Dale entertained Rodney with recollections of his former supervisor's wife, Delia Hodge. "Quite a beauty she was, Rodney. And no doubt still is. I'll bet that was her in the window yesterday, now that I think about it. Too bad I didn't get a better look. Still, I'd bet anything on it … that is, if I had anything to bet," he said, somehow erasing his doubts of the previous day regarding the mysterious face in the window of the house across the street from the lumberyard.

"In good weather she used to bring Randy his lunch in a brown poke along with a big green thermos filled with ice water or sometimes lemonade in the summer and always hot coffee in the winter. Big ole thermos, it was. Everybody kidded him about it. He'd meet Delia at the front gate. And when he did, all of us guys would watch … and not looking at his big thermos, either.

"In the summer Delia would come across the street wearing short shorts. When she wore dresses, which wasn't often, she always seemed a bit chunky for some reason. The way they fit her, I guess. She's a bit short and stocky. But in shorts, Lord God! Especially this one pair of orange ones she liked to wear with a tight yellow halter top. She looked just great in that outfit, and you could tell she knew it. She also knew all of us guys were watching her. Had to know it. And Randy knew it, too. I think he's the one that made her bring him his lunch just to show her off to the rest of us. As if to say, *look how lucky I am, boys.* He'd take the thermos and the poke from her and then give her a big smooch.

"He could just as easily have brought his damn lunch and thermos with him in the mornings, after all, just like the rest of us had to. But no! He had to have his wife bring him his and then give her a hug and a big kiss. Have her walk that meal across the street for him so's every guy could see her come and go. Front and back views! Well, we liked them both.

"But ole man Badgett liked looking at her, too. Saw him do it many times, looking at her from his office window. We used to say

41

that's how Randy must have got his job as supervisor—by promising Badgett that Delia would put on a show for him every day. And damned if she didn't, whether she meant to or not. Left on his own, Randy was no more a supervisor than any of the rest of us. Didn't know more and never worked any harder. Just had a wife with a lot to show, and that made the difference as far as we could tell."

Before Dale's descriptions of Delia Hodge became even more graphic, Rodney reached up and pulled the signal cord. Their bus stop was just ahead.

After a half-mile hike from the bus stop, they arrived at the junkyard and another chain link fence. This one was ten feet tall and topped with barbed wire. Sections of thin wooden slats were woven through the fencing to block the view of the yard's contents along the highway.

"So, how do we get in?" Dale asked. "Thought you said there wasn't much security here."

"We get in just like we did at your lumberyard. There's a gate in the back here, and there's no barbed wire over that gate, since that's where we received deliveries. Not only that, but the fence in the back doesn't have these slats. No need to block the view back there. So, out front it looks as though there is security, but in the back, not so. I should be able to climb right over the gate. Of course, that means we can only take items small enough to pass through the fence or carry back over the gate."

And after they walked to the rear fence, Rodney did, indeed, scale the fence with ease. He pulled himself up the gate and swung his lanky legs over the top more easily than he could have imagined before dropping to the ground on the other side. He had worried for some time about what the lack of exercise other than walking the streets might be doing to his overall health, especially his muscle tone. Now he was pleased with himself.

Once over the fence, he pulled from his pocket the bill of materials that Dale had given him and began walking toward the yard's office while Dale waited at the gate, holding two empty canvas carpenter's bags they had found in the lumberyard.

Little had changed in the yard since Rodney had last seen it. Walking toward the office, he thought again, as he had many times before, of just how much the junkyard's contents reflected the changing nature of the town and the country. Before the Greater Depression began, the yard mostly contained automobiles in various states of wreckage. But no longer. Now Rodney walked past large appliances—refrigerators and ovens, pedestal fans, and pallets stacked with PCs and microwave ovens and window air conditioner units—most covered with tarps fastened down with bungee cords. No one was available now to repair the PCs or ACs, and there were no new homes being built, so little need for the appliances, even ones that worked. The autos had long since gone for parts and then to scrap metal recyclers once the useable parts had been stripped from them and sold. With so few new autos in use to replace the old ones, automobiles had gradually disappeared from the streets and now even from junkyards.

He wondered what changes lay ahead. What set of people would become obsolete next in the inexorable devolution of living conditions brought on by the Federation's socialism? In the Happy Times there had been a sense of order derived from merit and market value. Now everything that could still be wrung from the tattered fabric of the new society soon evaporated into parity and was lost.

Entering the junkyard office was easy enough; Rodney found it unlocked. Who robs an out of business junkyard, after all? What's more, who cares if someone does? Rodney's boss had certainly not left any money behind. And most of the objects the yard contained were too large to steal or not worth taking, at least not for general use.

Inside the yard's tool cabinet Rodney carefully gathered up the items on the bill of materials: hammers, saws, screwdrivers of different kinds and sizes, and a set of wrenches, English not metric, though uncertain if they would be needed. Except for the saws, he stuffed all the tools in the canvas bag he carried, which was now too heavy to transport readily and inconspicuously back to the lumberyard for use. They would have to divide up the tools, just as they had expected, some going into the bags Dale was holding. Then they could get back on the bus. Still, everything had to be passed singly either through the gate's chain links or around its margins.

The carpenter's handsaws, however, were not so readily concealed. Rodney looked about for a way to disguise them and found old newspapers and a roll of tape at the yard's sales counter. He wrapped the saws in the newspapers along with pieces of cardboard to conceal their shape, turning them into long thin rectangles. Then he taped the wrappings shut. Once he'd gathered all the items on his list, including the brackets he thought might work with the barrels, Rodney lugged his haul back to the gate and passed the items to Dale, a few at a time, through the spaces between the gate and the fenceposts before scaling the fence again.

After riding the bus back to Southside, they hid the tools in one of the lumberyard sheds. Now they were beginning to feel optimistic about their project. The image of the completed shantyboat, brought to life by Rodney's crude sketches, gleamed in the sun on the little river of their imaginations. They now had what they needed to build their own shelter—access to lumber, tools, and fasteners. They were ready to begin.

Chapter 8: Boat Building

Now the two men had the work of shantyboat building to occupy their days. Jobs in private industry were scarce all across the country once the Greater Depression began—that is, jobs independent of Federation control, jobs that created economic value through the manufacture of a product or the performance of a service for which the public would be willing to pay a price that varied according to the interplay of supply, quality, and demand as the free market, on its own accord, sorted out economic value. With all private employment crushed under successive waves of Federation registration, regulation, taxation, and ultimately, when deemed necessary, confiscation, the public free market had died, killed off by these exigencies of the Federation's planned economy.

In a sense, consumers, too, were abolished as an economic factor, since they could no longer express their preferences in the marketplace through their purchases from a range of goods and services, because choice itself was gone. Instead, people could only purchase what the Federation permitted to be produced, mostly through forced prison labor. The results had gradually become more and more insufficient in both quality and quantity, much to the dissatisfaction of the Federation's citizens, who found that their opinions, whether political or commercial, were now completely ignored.

To keep the labor camps operating and thus producing a restricted flow of even inferior goods and services, the Federation needed a reliable supply of new prisoners. In order to create that supply and protect the Federation from a growing discontent that might at any time break into rioting across the country, the definitions of criminal activity had to be expanded to include mild or even suspected criticism of Federation officials and Federation policies. Such changes in the criminal code were, after all, necessitated by the greater good of the country's citizens. Such was the Federation's official position.

Convictions for sedition, for example, resulted from the flimsiest of evidence—informer reports, rumors, hearsay, mistaken identities—or even no evidence at all other than baseless claims and declarations by Federation officials. After a decades-long trend of leniency for the most criminal activity, even including the most vicious crimes, the punishments for these non-violent political crimes were now extended, often doubled, in many cases becoming tantamount to life sentences, for what previously had been legitimate expressions of American free speech.

The final blow to personal freedom for many citizens came with the confiscation of their property, both liquid and fixed assets. The progression of the Federation's desperate measures had become clear: first, taxation and regulation destroyed businesses, especially the smaller, more vulnerable ones. That action in turn created a massive increase in unemployment, which in a knock-on effect actually decreased tax revenues. And that decrease in tax revenues more than outweighed any increase in Federation revenues from regulation fines and penalties.

After the Federation reached the limits of taxation and regulation, having already taxed most individuals and businesses into desperation yet still finding itself short of adequate revenues, the Federation began to seize the property of both businesses and individuals through foreclosures implemented by the banks, which the Federation now for all practical purposes controlled entirely.

Next, after outlawing cash-only transactions, the Federation began freezing the bank accounts of its target victims, beginning with its known political opponents, once again utilizing its control over the banking system to do so. The government then liquidated the frozen accounts through secret transfers to various Federation accounts.

Its insatiable need for money still not satisfied, the Federation last of all began seizing any remaining private property, typically utilizing false claims of overdue taxes or unpaid fines. Both businesses and individuals became targets, starting once again with the Federation's known opponents. But as the government's needs continued to grow faster than its revenues, confiscations began to affect the general population. Once confiscations began, the Federation quickly became dependent upon them and so began liquidating the accounts and possessions of even its own previously ardent supporters, leaving untouched only the properties of the Federation officials themselves.

In this way, the Federation continued to fund its enormous expansion of spending programs that provided subsistence to the legions of vagrants that it had itself created, thus transforming the nation into a vast welfare state of citizens unable to resist the government controls thrust upon them, controls on which their continued existence now seemed completely to depend. What the Federation lost in the process, however, was nearly all its popular support—partially to vagrancy and partially to resentment over the ever-increasing burden of supporting the unemployed.

All these activities the Federation masked with the pretense of compassion. First, the Federation created a crisis, as often as not intentionally, and then used that crisis as a pretext to seize, under the ruse of compassion and national emergency, more power and more capital and restrict more and more of the freedoms of its citizens until few were left. In this way, all the frogs in the national kettle came to a slow but inevitable boil.

Openly objecting to confiscations or any other of the Federation's "compassionate" actions, by either individuals or businesses, was treated as sedition and punished promptly and ruthlessly. The Federation Police arrested objectors, often without the formality of warrants, raiding their homes in the middle of the night, tearing their dwellings to shreds in the search for anything that might serve as evidence of sedition, even though evidence was not really needed. Speedy trials followed, usually within days, and lasted only a few minutes before the gavel of justice rapped, thus ending the freedoms of the accused. The few victims who still knew world history noted similarities between these Federation proceedings and the Jacobin trials during the Reign of Terror that quickly followed the French Revolution. Moreover, the rapping gavel seemed similar to the crash of the guillotine's blade on the necks of the accused, whether royal or common, wealthy or poor. The only protected class now was those who supported the Parity Party and made a public display of that support. But for anyone to raise objections to the Party's and, therefore, the Federation's policies was now in effect a suicidal act.

After their trials came speedy transportation of the newly convicted to the work camps where their labor had already been scheduled. The sentences of the convicted were often for an indefinite term. Their families were always told that the terms of confinement were for five years or until the seditionist confessed his political sins and gave evidence of reform. The Federation avoided defining "evidence of reform," and no one, it seems, ever adequately confessed or reformed. Thus, in practice, the families of the convicted never heard from their loved ones again. And so, they too, the families of these alleged seditionists, whether young or old, women or children, often having lost their only source of livelihood to this judicial process, soon joined the vast roiling sea of vagrants.

To become employed again, a vagrant's best chance was to work as a staff member in one of the canteens or shelters, cooking the food, ladling it out, changing the beds, laundering and repairing the soiled clothing, cleaning the shower rooms. A few others might gain work in the public transit system issuing tokens, driving buses, or cleaning and servicing them. Or they might work in other public services—sanitation, utilities, medical service, or clerical administration in government offices. But with even the most menial of these jobs, a guardian angel was required—someone of influence within the local Parity Party leadership, someone who could obtain an application form and guide it, once completed with key signal words and phrases, through the successive obstacles of race, gender, ethnicity, and, most of all, verified political affiliation, and thus shepherd the application through the Federation's narrow gates of employment.

For higher level positions, such as administrative managers or police officers, the Federation recruited candidates, not from public applications, but silently, in secret, from private lists supplied by the Parity Party and its network of donors and friends. Thus, for the majority of vagrants, ones such as Dale and Rodney, there were no angels to guide them and, therefore, no gates of employment to swing open and welcome them. But now, in defiance of the Federation and its distended powers, Dale and Rodney did have a job, albeit a surreptitious one. In the shrinking September daylight, they were building a shantyboat.

The exertion of hauling supplies from the yard to the riverbank under the early autumn sun prompted them each day to shed their shirts. Seeing himself in the river water, Rodney was reminded of pictures of the dispossessed of Appalachia he had seen in a sociology class he had once taken—people emaciated in the torso and gaunt in the face with sunken cheeks but still retaining the spark of humanity in their eyes—and all of this exaggerated in Rodney's case by his height. Dale, on the other hand, though he had grown thinner, was still by far the more muscular of the two. In fact, his newly acquired thinness only served to emphasize his abdominal muscles. His was still the sort of male body schoolgirls dreamed about and whispered about to each other in closed furtive circles.

Then, suddenly, Rodney laughed.

"What's so damn funny?" Dale asked with a playful smirk after removing his shirt. "You're no beauty, either, you know."

"Oh, I know I'm not. I can see that in the river water here," he said while still looking at his reflection. "But I was just thinking. When we're changing in the Rag Room or taking showers, we all look a bit like this—at least most guys do once they've been walking the streets for a while. There we don't think much of it, but standing here face-to-face in the sunlight makes it really personal. So sad that it's funny, I guess you could say. But this is what we've become. No hiding it here. The good part is, as we get this project going, we'll rebuild our bodies. Obviously, I need to do that a lot more than you do. But as we work, then we'll have to worry about someone asking us how we got our muscles and our tans, thinking they'll want to do the same. Or a curious snitch might just try to follow us to find out what we're up to!"

Risks or not, once started, they descended on their project with the fervor of great savage birds of prey, talons extended, falling on some helpless lesser creature, and growing more and more pleased with themselves as they did and less and less patient with delays and setbacks, for the declining autumn sun reminded them each day just how much they needed to hurry their work along. Further, just as Rodney predicted, their muscles did indeed gradually return.

But those larger, restored muscles were accompanied by increased hunger that forced them to filch food as often as they could from the canteen or anywhere else they could find it. A certain amount of theft—an extra slice of bread today, an extra drink tomorrow—was expected and tolerated by the canteen employees who would simply ignore it when the guards weren't nearby, but it was another risk the men were taking.

First on the project punch list they'd devised was the building of the deck. On the bank of the little river just below the lumberyard, they laid it out in a nearly level area, following Rodney's drawings. A rectangular frame of two-by-eights, reinforced in the corners with galvanized brackets, then covered with six-inch planks. All fastened together under the morning and noontime sun and completed six days later in the afternoon shade provided by a large willow tree that sheltered their work. Having to do all the sawing and drilling by hand, as time-consuming as that was, produced a minimal amount of noise. Besides, no electricity was available along the riverbank where they worked, nor was there electricity any longer in the lumberyard itself.

After the deck came the barrels. They carried them one at a time to the river and banged their lids on as tightly as they could with a rubber mallet the yard had kept for that purpose. Then they applied a silicone sealant Rodney had found at the junk yard. They tested each barrel by rolling up their pant legs and floating the barrel into the river's shallows. There they would force the barrels down into the water and rotate them slowly, watching for air bubbles. Two barrels had to be dried out in the sun and resealed before they became serviceable.

They made several more trips to the junkyard, one for better brackets to fasten the drums to the underside of the deck and one for tools they hadn't thought of. Rodney thought they would need a rudder for the stern of the shanty just in case they had to relocate it, but they had no way to transport such a large and conspicuous item. Besides, these trips cost them more time than they could spare.

After completing the shanty's flat-bottomed hull and sealing the blue barrels, they fastened them to the underside of the deck with the brackets from the junkyard. But after heaving the deck upside down to secure the barrels, they realized that they would have to move it into the water now in order to complete the project. Otherwise, with only the strength of the two of them, they would not be able to move the shanty at all once the cabin was built on the deck.

They managed to flip the deck into the water thanks more to the riverbank's slope than to their own effort, but even then accomplished the feat only after sliding, both of them, into the river as part of the launch. The deck atop the barrels hit the river with a tremendous splash while its builders tumbled in after it. There they sat in the river shallows, drenched, watching the deck bob before them, laughing at both their good fortune and their mishap, for the deck, in its moment of truth, floated, whereupon the two men risked raising a modest cheer that could have been heard from the street, had anyone been there to hear them.

Next the cabin had to be built in sections on the bank and then moved and installed on the deck. Still, as much as possible, they avoided hammering. But as October also began to slip away, they realized that they would, indeed, need to use nails at least on the cabin superstructure in order to finish before the onset of winter. Hand drilling for wood screws, though much quieter, simply took too long. They would just have to incur the risk of their hammer blows ringing on nail heads being heard along the street above. The shortening of the time to complete the project forced them to take on these additional risks.

Chapter 9: Murder

The autumn days were waning now, more noticeably each day. The shadows of the trees along the riverbank lengthened sooner each afternoon as if the sun's only purpose were to remind the men of its inevitable retreat to the south. *Soon*, it seemed to be telling them, *I'll withdraw my support and punish any delinquents with work still undone.* The men hammered away, heedless now of how much noise they made. They still went shirtless most days, showing their reconstituted physiques defiantly to the sun as the shanty's superstructure took shape.

One day when the cabin walls were up and they were at work on the roof beams, Dale spent much of the morning fretting about a vagrant who had been staring at them during breakfast in the Southside canteen. No amount of hammering or sawing could stop his grousing.

"The guy could be a rat, you know. Never can tell." Dale kept up his complaining with variations on the theme of treachery all morning. "He sure seemed odd to me. Kept staring at us. Didn't you see him?" No, Rodney hadn't noticed.

Finally, Dale stopped to get a drink from one of the water bottles they had taken from the canteen. Having no other way to cool their water, they simply left the bottles in the shade of their project helpmate, the willow tree along the riverbank. They had frequently retreated to its refreshing shade during their boatbuilding that summer. By now, it seemed like a close friend.

Dale crossed from the shanty to the riverbank over the sturdy plank they had secured for this purpose. He stood in the willow's shade now, near the plank, taking a long draft from the water bottle before commenting, "Warm as piss, as always. But better than no water at all, I suppose."

Rodney watched him for a moment, thinking he, too, might as well get a drink, and started to walk across the plank. But as he was about to step onto the riverbank, he saw Dale tense up. Hearing something, Dale whirled around to his right, then stepped out from the willow's shade, continuing to look off to his right, upriver, without saying anything. He stood there, frozen, listening hard, holding the bottle a few inches from his open mouth, his eyes wide with concern. Rodney stopped, as well, with one foot still on the plank. They both listened, stiff as statues.

Then came a rustling of leaves and branches, faint but audible. And not caused by the wind, for there was no wind this morning. Then more noise, louder this time, as though close by someone might have slipped and fallen on the bank, which was still wet from the previous day's thundershower. Dale slowly recapped his bottle while still staring in the direction of the sounds. Then, seeing something, he threw the bottle to the ground, snatched up the hammer he had carried ashore, and yelled to Rodney, "Damn spy, I'll bet. And there he goes!" With that, he raced diagonally across the riverbank, tearing through the underbrush toward the noise.

Then Rodney could see a man emerge from the brush, flushed like a rabbit by a hound, breaking for the corner of the lumberyard's fence, where it started steeply uphill toward Camden Avenue. But Dale's rapid start and diagonal path across the bank allowed him to intercept the man, who was struggling to go straight up the hillside. Before the man could reach the corner of the lumberyard's fence, Dale grabbed him by the collar and pulled him backward onto the ground. There they both tumbled into the brush and out of Rodney's view for a moment. But within a moment more, Rodney could see the rapid rise and fall of Dale's hammer above the shrubbery and, as he drew nearer, could hear the man cry out as the hammer thudded on his skull again and again and then one last time. By the time Rodney reached them, the struggle had ended decisively. Dale, the victor, the bloody hammer still in his hand, rose from the ground to stand over his victim.

"Good God, Dale, what have you done!"

"Killed a damn spy, that's what I've done," he said, breathless now but proud. "It was him or us, Rodney, him or us, no choice to it, just him or us. A damn rat, that's what he was. I knew it all the time just by looking at him in the canteen. I knew it. It's the same damn guy, Rodney, the one I saw at the canteen this morning, the one staring at us." Dale finally caught his breath before adding, "Now here he lies! Take a good look for yourself. He's a damn dead rat now."

Rodney did look, peering reluctantly over the crushed shrubbery. What he saw was a face covered in blood, gripped by agony, and a head distorted by partial collapse on the left side from the hammer blows.

"He would have squealed on us for sure, Rodney, just to wrap himself in some nice clothes and wolf down a big meal. That's what the sonofabitch was up to. You can bet on that. Well, he won't squeal now!"

"No, he definitely won't do that," Rodney replied calmly, trying to assuage Dale's anger. "But what are we going to do with what's left of him?"

"We have to take care that his corpse doesn't manage to squeal on us, that's what. Got that big pocketknife of yours on you?"

"Always do. Here it is." Rodney reached into his hip pocket. "Why? What are you going to do with it?"

"Slice off this guy's right ear, that's what. Figure we can wrap it in something and throw it away farther downriver toward the canteen and shelter. Maybe do it when we go that way this evening. But want to cut it off right now, so's we don't forget about it."

"Okay," Rodney replied, still trying to be the calmer of the two, as he handed over the knife, albeit somewhat reluctantly. "But what about the body? What do you propose we do with that?"

"Throw it in the damn river," Dale said with a grunt as he pulled the man's ear taut and cut it off, then squeezed the now bloody lobe repeatedly to be sure he had gotten the microchip.

"The river?"

'Yeah, got to put it in the river. Say, you seem kind of shaky about this, Rodney. You okay?"

"Well, you realize that if we get caught now, we could be in for a lot more trouble than just a few months of hard labor because we were building a shanty and doing it with stolen material. If the police find out about this guy, it's a life of hard labor for the both of us and most likely a short life at that."

"So, what was I supposed to do, just let this rat run away and blab to the authorities? He's a damn spy, Rodney. An informer. Can't you see that! And now he got just what he deserved! We got to get some cable, not rope that'll rot, but wire of some kind and wind it around him with something heavy attached. Then we'll pull him out to the center of the river and let him sink. I can do it. If he should bob up later for some damn reason, before the carp and catfish pick his bones clean, at least we'd be the ones most likely to spot him and have time to do something about it."

"Okay, what's done is done, I guess. We've got no other choice now. But let's hurry. Just in case he had someone waiting for him up at the street and that person decides to come down here to check on him."

"We'll take a look around along the street when we go up there to get the wire and some weights, but I doubt he was going to share his spy reward with anyone. Come on, let's go now."

Dale was right; no one was on the street. So, they proceeded to dispose of the body by wrapping it in a length of wire fencing they'd found to which they attached a vise they removed from the yard's workshop. Dale, stripped naked, managed to swim the body far enough from shore for it to sink out of sight in the middle of the river. On the way to the shelter that night, Dale disposed of the ear by tossing it to a stray dog. "Good luck to anybody who wants to trace the signal from that earlobe," Dale quipped. "No telling where it will end up next."

Chapter 10: Walter Badgett

After the murder, several weeks went by without another incident. By then the roof was shingled, leaving only the outfitting of the interior of the cabin before completion of the project.

Pressing hard now to complete their work, the men finished the shanty by late October in every respect save one—namely, the installation of a stove. They managed their project despite delays from a week of unexpected rains that forced them to spend time trapped inside the lumberyard's sheds just waiting for the rain to stop, unable to do anything useful and thus losing entire days of progress to the rain and mud. Nevertheless, the cabin now bobbed before them, perched on the shanty's deck, bathed in autumn sunshine. It featured two sliding windows they had removed from a deserted house and placed on either side of the cabin above the built-in bunks. An oak exterior door faced the shanty's bow. They had also taken a door from one of the neighborhood's abandoned homes of which by now there were many to choose from.

In addition to stealing building materials, they had also taken mattresses and blankets from empty homes to supply the two small bunks they had built inside the cabin. All of these ventures required them to forsake nights in the community shelter in order to raid the abandoned homes during the night, carry their prizes back to the shanty in the darkness, and then spend the night sleeping in the yard's sheds, hoping they would not be discovered by a guard they continued to fear but had never yet encountered.

Finally, with the bunks and bedding in place, they were able to sleep in the shantyboat—an accomplishment that brought them greater pleasure than anything since losing their own families and homes.

They thought of their foraging adventures into the surrounding neighborhood as entirely justified. They were simply recycling items that would otherwise be lost to the Federation, since the abandoned houses would eventually be emptied, their contents junked or taken and reused by other desperate vagrants like themselves, and the houses set ablaze either by squatters trying to survive the winter or demolished by Federation authorities as unsightly fire and health hazards, which they truly had become. Many of the houses the men investigated in their foraging were already rat-infested and structurally damaged by nature's intrusions through leaking roofs or broken windows. This deterioration process was a well-established pattern in other towns across the country by this stage of the Greater Depression from which, after ten years, no path of escape had yet emerged. As for the murder of the suspected informer, neither of them mentioned it again, not to each other and certainly not to anyone else.

The men had fitted the shanty's walls for winter with insulation they found stored in the yard's third shed, the one beyond the office building. In their minds, their use of these materials, just like their foraging in abandoned houses, in no way constituted theft, since there was little chance of the materials ever being sold now anyway. Such was their repeated rationalization about their appropriation of materials and supplies.

Still, taking the insulation had been their biggest risk to date, greater even than the murder of the spying vagrant. Because the rolls of insulation were so large, there was no concealing any longer that material was missing, at least from the third shed. In the other two sheds, they had been careful to spread out the remaining inventory as they removed decking and framing materials in order to decrease the likelihood of their "borrowings" being detected.

In this and other ways, some great and some small, their risks had mounted up as the shanty project progressed toward its completion. And did so despite their ever present concern for concealment and deception. Nevertheless, they had managed their project so far without detection by a security guard or the lumberyard owner or by Federation police. They had not, for example, encountered any guard inspecting the lumberyard during the day, nor had they found any evidence of a guard's inspection overnight.

Now the only remaining task to complete their project was to remove the antique stove and stove piping from the yard office and install it in the shanty. Wood to burn in it was plentiful along the little river's shoreline. Thus, the promise of a warm bed of their own during the winter and occasional hot food and drink of their own choosing seemed possible once again. Not the same as having a home and family perhaps but something of their own, nevertheless. And what's more, the shanty was something created by their own hands from their own initiative and labor rather than being a gift from the Federation's binding charity, which had more the quality of flypaper than compassion. Even the shanty's small freedoms, amid such great deprivations as now surrounded them, had quickly become precious to them.

They managed to remove the stove, heavy and bulky though it was, slide it down the hill to the shanty, and lug it aboard. Inside the cabin they had already built a platform and a wall shield of used bricks to absorb and thus prolong the stove's heat while at the same time protecting the deck and plywood wall. The final piece of this project was the removal of the stove pipe from inside and outside the office. They deliberately left this task to the very end, since afterward there would be no way to conceal what they had done. Anyone familiar with the office would be able to tell at a glance, even from the street, that the piping was missing. And this fact, they knew, required them to move the shanty as soon as possible upstream to an inlet they'd found bordered by overarching willows. There, they believed, the shanty would be less visible from both sides of the river, even during the leafless winter.

After installing the stove and its piping, the two sat in a grassy patch of the riverbank, stretching themselves after the strain of their labors. They drank two white wine coolers they had managed to filch from the rear of a delivery truck to celebrate the end of their achievement. The early November day was warm and dry. The shanty now sat calmly in the river's low waters awaiting the winter rains.

"Glad we don't have that much work left, Rodney. Just tidying up a bit," Dale said with a sigh of relief. "That damn stove might be little, but it's heavy."

"Yes, it sure is, but now it's in place." Rodney sighed and then added, "It's all done."

"And that stove makes the cabin look real cozy. Even the stove pipe looks good. Next we need to try out the stove. But right now, just look at her—the whole shantyboat! She hardly moves on the water, just enough to rock you to sleep."

And amazing as it seemed, there before them bobbed the shantyboat they'd built together, splendid in their view. The blue fifty-five-gallon barrels sealed against the river's floods were fastened to the underside of the deck. The deck itself was a sturdy, neatly trimmed rectangle accessed via a wide two-by-eight plank.

The plank was spiked into the river's perpetually muddy bank and tied at the other end to a cleat on the shanty's deck—a cleat taken from a junked sailboat. Covering the cabin was a slightly pitched and shingled roof, a patchwork of blue, brown, and grey shingles they had sorted through to find uniform size and sufficient quality. Windows were on both sides of the cabin. And shading the cabin's interior were Roman blinds the men had taken along with the windows when they raided an abandoned house three blocks away. A narrow door to the fore of the cabin also sported a small window at head height. A small enclosure with a seat overhanging the stern to the starboard side served as their privy. And now, protruding from the rear of the cabin was the stovepipe, raising its tiny rain cap just above the roof's peak.

Inside the cabin the men had built two bunks, no more than three feet wide, leaving another three-foot space between them as an aisleway leading from the door to the stove at the rear of the cabin, no more than twelve feet long. The remaining space to the fore of each bunk on both sides as well as the space beneath the bunks served for the storage of their meager possessions, mostly stolen fruits and other food they had found and clothing, especially socks and spare shoes they'd managed to find, for in these desperate times stray items were regarded as treasures.

But the most valuable feature of the shanty was the stolen antique stove. It was small but tasteful in its workmanship, with metal coils and fancy rosettes welded to its surface in an intricate display of vulcan art. Now it stood at the rear of their shanty's cabin awaiting the first charge of wood which it would consume to protect the men against the winter's freezing grip. To offset the weight of the stove and relevel the deck, they had filled two of their canvas carpenter bags with sand and placed them on either side of the cabin entrance.

Dale leaned back on his elbows and mused, "I wonder how ole Noah felt when he finished his ark and started marching the animals inside. Suppose he felt anything like we're feeling right now?"

"Satisfaction, you mean?"

"Yes, indeed, just that—satisfaction. We've prepared for the winter just like ole Noah prepared for the storm."

"I think he must have but with one big difference," Rodney offered.

"Oh?" Dale sat up again, a bit alarmed. "And what's that?"

"Noah knew what was going to happen next, to him, his family, and the animals. We, on the other hand, have no idea what will happen to us. God warned Noah, gave him a detailed survival plan, and allowed him time to prepare for the Flood. But we have no idea what will happen next to us but suspect it won't be good, since nothing else has been for a long time. Have we built a makeshift temple to our freedom or a tomb? There's no way to know for sure, but we do know that we've tried for freedom and along the way committed some terrible crimes and taken some great risks."

They fell silent, mulling over the truth of Rodney's comments, staring at the shanty and listening to the river's soothing voice lapping at the riverbank.

"Well, we should try it out," Dale said, finally breaking the spell as they sat admiring their work—this masterpiece of ingenuity, resourcefulness, and theft inspired by their desire for personal freedom.

"The stove you mean?" Rodney asked, and Dale nodded.

"Yes. Yes, I think we should," Rodney replied as he turned on his side to push himself upright.

But before he could take so much as a single step toward the woods to search for kindling, a voice boomed out from above them, "So, this is it! So, this is where my lumber's gone to, is it?"

Recognizing the voice immediately, Dale whirled around to face his boss, Walter Badgett, who stood on the hillside, halfway between them and the lumberyard's rear gate, close enough to see both the men and their shanty, and being himself large enough in every respect to overshadow them.

"Oh, God!" The words leaped from Dale's mouth involuntarily.

"And you're the one who's done it. Damn you, Dale! I always thought you were an incompetent clown, but I never took you for a thief, as well. So, this is my reward for giving you a job and keeping you on to the very end to help you and your family—you steal from me! Even took my precious antique stove from my office, did you? I paid a lot of money for that stove and not so that you two could warm your scrawny behinds with it this winter! Community shelters aren't good enough for the two of you, huh? No, you have to go and steal from somebody on top of all the public money a few of us already pay to shelter and feed the worthless likes of you two."

Rodney gave a quick glance at Dale, expecting him to reply. But the appearance of this raging creature halfway up the hill, lording above them, rendered Dale white, slack-faced, and dumbstruck. Rodney now stared up at Badgett, whose plump reddened jowls were quivering with emotion.

"And my guard, Ellis—he was in on this, too, wasn't he, Dale? Helping you take my lumber out of the sheds? Selling some of it, I suppose, while you were all at it? Otherwise, I don't see how he could have missed all that you've stolen, not if he were really making inspections. Good thing I've finally come here myself. Now I see for myself what's been happening."

"We never saw your guard," Rodney finally answered for Dale, "and he wasn't in on anything we've done."

"Never saw him, huh? Well, I might believe you on that part. Regardless, I've already dealt with Ellis. But by God, now I'll see to it that the two of you are sent to the worst labor camp in the entire country! That'll be your next shelter, not that shantyboat! Even stole my antique stove and its piping, did you? Well, we'll just see what that brings you. You two will work like you've never worked before in your entire lives in the camp they'll send you to. I'll see to it. And you'll deserve every grueling day of it, too. And there you'll die— the both of you. Die in your misery, just as you deserve. I'll get the Federation police down here right now to see all of this, to see all that you've done to me, and once they do, away you two will go, never to return!"

But Rodney replied, "I think you better reconsider that, Mr. Badgett."

"Hah, me reconsider! You two should have reconsidered what you were doing before stealing my lumber. Reconsidered long and hard. My lumberyard may have closed, but all this material is still mine, and this hill I'm standing on is mine, and that bank you two are standing on is mine, and all the material you've stolen to make that damn shantyboat is mine. I may not be in business as I was, but I still know people in this town, people who will see to it that you get the punishment you deserve, the both of you. So there, Mister whatever your name is, there you have my reconsideration. You two should long ago have reconsidered what you've been doing. But it's too late now. As for my guard, I obviously wasted my time and money on him, but I've already taken care of him, whether he was

61

in with you or not. And now, by damn, I'll take care of the two of you, also. I'm calling the police and calling them right now."

"Don't do that," Rodney warned again in a voice still even and calm but honed now to a sharp edge of malice. "That wouldn't be wise, Mr. Badgett, not wise at all. What's done is done. Just let it go. Compared to everything else that's going on in the world around us, what we've done here is a minor thing. Your lumber wasn't being used for anything else and, though you may not be willing to admit it yet, none of it ever will be again, at least not by you. If anyone, the Federation will sell it—those same people you trust to help you punish us. So, you'd be smarter by far just to forget about all this and be glad nothing worse has happened."

"Now listen here, I won't be lectured to by a damn thief!" Badgett had his phone in his hand now, waving it at Rodney. "There's no way I'm going to just ignore what you two have done to me. And you, Dale, why are you just standing there like a damn fool and letting this man speak for you? Is he the one who got you into this mess in the first place? I don't believe you ever could think for yourself."

Searching vainly for a reply, Dale only managed to shuffle his feet a bit and stammer incoherently. But Rodney, his eyes still fastened on Walter Badgett and his phone, spoke again. "Listen to what I just told you, old man. You should know by now that snitches come to a bad end, and fast. So, put that phone away before you regret it." Rodney took a step up the hill as he spoke to ensure that Badgett understood the gravity of his remarks.

As Rodney approached with his hands behind his back, it finally did occur to Walter Badgett that perhaps, just perhaps, he did not have the upper hand here, that, in fact, there might be danger, real danger, for himself. That these men had created something they felt worth defending, even to the point of violence. At least this one stepping toward him now seemed to feel that way. Badgett stared for a long moment at the man's impassive face, wondering what the man would do. Then he heard the click of a knife blade locking into place. Next he saw the glint of its blade in the rays of the afternoon sun that had found their way through the shade of the willows and sycamores along the riverbank. Rodney continued to approach, both of his hands in clear view now, holding a knife in one of them.

Instantly, Walter Badgett's rage dissolved into a flood of panic. He turned and tried to run up the hill, back to his office, to barricade himself inside, he thought, to escape somehow to a place of safety and refuge. He tried, just as the spy before him had tried when Dale caught and killed him, hammering him to death. Older and heavier and weaker than Rodney, Walter Badgett had no chance. He was no more than a step inside his lumberyard's rear gate when the knife blade pierced his right kidney. He bellowed at first like a bison beset by wolves when it feels their first bites. Rodney's left hand quickly covered Badgett's mouth and muffled his cries while his right hand thrust the knife into Badgett's back twice more in rapid succession, finding with the last thrust the back door to his heart, dispatching him into immediate and permanent silence.

Badgett dropped straight down at Rodney's feet, still holding his partially dialed cellphone, blood gushing from his wounds. Because they were still on the hillside, the bulk of Badgett's dead weight immediately rolled up against Rodney's ankles, forcing him to brace himself by quickly moving his right foot downhill while trying to hold Badgett's corpse in place with his hands and left foot. "Come on, Dale," he cried out, "I need your help. This guy weighs a ton!"

"Great God, Rodney! What have you done?" Dale asked, finally recovering from his mental paralysis.

"What does it look like I've done? I've silenced a snitch, the same as you did."

"Yeah, but nobody ever missed my snitch. They'll notice this one for sure. He wasn't lying about knowing important people. Good God, just look at the blood coming from him!"

"Well, knowing important people didn't save his lumberyard, and it hasn't saved him, either."

"I can see that, but it won't be long before someone comes looking for him, and they'll know just where to look."

"Maybe they'll come, maybe they won't. Either way, he's dead now, and we need to dispose of his body just the way we did with your spy. So, let's get to it."

They carefully rolled Badgett's corpse to the bottom of the bank, leaving a trail of blood as they did. After placing the body on a nearly level spot, they gathered some more wire fencing and, stripping Badgett of his wallet and wristwatch (his shoes and other clothes were too large for either of them), they wrapped his corpse in the fencing together with some large stones. Once again, Dale, by far the better swimmer, towed the corpse to the middle of the river and let it sink. Rodney smashed the phone with a hammer and threw it into the river, as well, but saved Badgett's wristwatch for Dale. He would later burn the wallet.

"Damn, that water's cold now!" Dale said after coming ashore, shivering uncontrollably.

Rodney quickly put a towel around him. "Dry yourself really well, Dale. We can't afford to have you get sick. Besides, now we definitely have to move the shanty upstream before the police come looking for Badgett. And we also need to wash away his blood from the hillside."

The price of their freedom rose that afternoon from one life to two.

Chapter 11: Investigation

Moving the shanty upstream, even with the river's flow near its seasonal low level, proved to be an arduous task. They knew it would be. In fact, despite the risk, they devoted two days to it, trusting in the laxity of the Federation police to respond only belatedly to Walter Badgett's disappearance. On the morning of the second day they managed to pull the shanty beneath the shelter of two willows whose branches arched out over a narrow bank. Now they overhung the shanty, as well, extending in all a quarter of the small river's width toward the north shore. Even without their leaves, the branches seemed to the men like the thousand arms of a welcoming crowd just set free from long captivity, arms that reached out to them in joyous acceptance. In the shelter of these willows they moored their new home again, using rebars this time, which they drove deep into the bank before lashing the mooring ropes to them. Next they set in place the plank they had brought along with them from their work site.

"Whew, that was a hell of a job to move the shanty up here, it really was!" Dale said as he slumped onto the deck and dangled his legs over the side with his heels coming to rest on one of the blue barrels.

Leaning back against the cabin beside Dale, Rodney replied, "Yes, but we left a clear trail of crushed shrubs and weeds and broken branches along the way. Anybody can see it from here if he cares to look." He pointed in the direction of the path they had made.

"But will they?" Dale offered. "No one comes down this way any more, as we've seen. Besides, the river will be rising soon when the winter rains come and the snow follows. Then our trail will just disappear. I'd say we have more to fear from someone spotting us from the other side of the river. I'm feeling better about our chances now that we've moved the shanty."

<hr>

What they didn't know was that the Federation police had already identified Walter Badgett's killer. Agnes Badgett had reported the disappearance of her husband when he failed to return from his inspection of the lumberyard.

"He probably ran into that guard he hired—Ellis Grant—as worthless a man as you could ever imagine," Agnes told the two detectives, who, along with an armed officer, finally came to the Badgett house, responding to her third call of the day, an ultimatum that time.

"Walter had already chewed him out, I can tell you that much," she said. "I heard him do it. That's why he went to inspect the yard, because he suspected this Grant character was shirking his duties, maybe even selling the materials for his own gain. And that's just what I think, too. Walter had seen that materials were missing from the storage sheds. He just didn't know how much without doing a full inventory. That's what he went to check on."

"I understand, Mrs. Badgett," said the lead detective, trying to assuage her anger.

"Well, what are you going to do about it? Grant was probably waiting in the lumberyard for my husband to arrive. We need to get down there to search for him. Walter may still be down there and injured. Probably is. Don't you understand the urgency of this?"

Agnes insisted on going along even though the detectives urged her to stay at home. "What we might find at the lumberyard could be disturbing," the second detective said. "There's no way to know."

"He's my husband, and it's our lumberyard, and I am going there to look for him, and that's that," Agnes declared emphatically. "And I'm going right now, with or without you. So there. Now, are you gentlemen coming along?"

They all went, the four of them. At the lumberyard, the detectives milled about, glancing in the storage sheds, inside the office building, and about the grounds, not knowing what they were looking at, scarcely knowing what to look for, and so offering no observations let alone conclusions.

"Well," Agnes finally asked after doing some inspecting of the yard herself, "what have you found? Anything?"

"We don't see any sign of your husband or of foul play," the lead detective replied.

"Oh, no? Well, didn't you see that hole in the wall of the office building? Did you miss something as obvious as that? There was a stove pipe there. Or do you think that all office buildings have holes in their walls? And what's this splattered on the ground here by the rear gate?" she asked as her always volatile temper rose nearer to the point of rage. "Check that soil for blood, why don't you? And look down the hill beyond the gate. There, look there! Can't you see those drag marks? Something heavy has been taken down there. Lots of things, it looks like to me. Go down there and investigate that, too," she fumed.

"But we don't have a key to unlock the gate," they pleaded.

"Well, I do." And with that declaration, Agnes opened the gate, whereupon the detectives sent the armed officer down the hill to investigate while they stayed behind, milling about some more, mostly to kill time.

"Can't you two go with him?" Agnes asked.

"We don't have any weapons," they replied. "Special permits are required for those, and we detectives don't have permits."

"You need special permits to do your job?" Agnes started to add, *Walter had a pistol, and I would have brought it along, had I known this.* But, mindful of the Great Confiscation that supposedly stripped everyone of privately owned guns, she instead resorted to, "Tell me this, do I have to investigate my husband's disappearance all by myself? Is policing a self-service activity now the way getting fuel in your vehicle used to be, when we still have vehicles, that is?"

"No, no, of course not," they assured her. "We'll take care of this."

"I'll bet if one of the Federation officials were missing, you'd be quick enough to investigate every possibility and look under every rock. You'd all be down there at the river right now, looking everywhere. But with a private citizen, even one who still pays taxes, you don't seem to care. We don't count, do we? Is that it? No matter how much we pay in taxes to keep you in your miserable jobs, we still don't count?"

The detectives launched into a lengthy explanation of the differences between crimes against the Federation, which, after all, affect everyone, and crimes against individuals, which have a lesser impact on society and, therefore, merit fewer of the Federation's resources. Their defenses, however, were interrupted by the sight of the police officer trudging back up the hill, his hand on his holster, more for effect than for cause.

"Nothing down there," he said. "No sign of a corpse, that's for sure." Then, seeing Mrs. Badgett's distraught face, he added, "Oops. Sorry, ma'am. Didn't mean any offense. Does look like some vagrants have been messing around down there and probably scratched around here trying to get in the back gate, but that's all. We find that kind of thing is pretty common, especially with businesses that have their backs to the river like this one, Mrs. Badgett."

The detectives launched back into their defensive arguments as though there had been no pause. Their explanations became increasingly convoluted with administrative details, constraining conditions, and overriding social concerns but remained consistently self-serving.

Exasperated, Agnes finally interrupted them. "Look, I don't care about these fine distinctions in your procedures right now. I want you to find my husband. Do you understand me? Now, tell me what you are going to do about this Ellis Grant character. And the answer better not be that he belongs to some newly protected identity group that is now exempt from prosecution no matter what heinous crimes they've committed. Do you understand me?"

"Oh, no, nothing like that," they assured her.

"Well, then, find Ellis Grant, and find out what he knows about what still seems to me to be blood on the soil here and drag marks going down the hillside. I'll bet he knows exactly what happened to Walter and where he is."

Agnes's venom-tipped prodding soon provided more than enough motivation for the detectives, who, while still in Agnes's presence, requested and received permission via a cell phone call to the local Federation prosecutor to arrest Ellis Grant.

Chapter 12: Interrogation

Interrogator: Your boss, Mr. Walter Badgett, did he ever criticize your work as a security guard?

Grant: Please, I don't know about these kinds of things. Can't I have a lawyer to help me?

Interrogator: Are you saying you don't trust the Federation?

Grant: No, I'm saying that I need help with something like this. Most people like me have no experience with being questioned about such a serious thing as murder.

Interrogator: Did I say there was a murder?

Grant: No, you didn't, but everyone is thinking that, since Mr. Badgett's been missing for what—five or six days now?

Interrogator: Why don't you tell me how many days Mr. Badgett has been missing? You know, don't you?

Grant: No, no, I don't for sure. See, you're trying to trip me up already. At least let me talk to a lawyer. The Federation owes legal help to everyone, doesn't it?

Interrogator: Not any more. Besides, if you didn't kill Walter Badgett, then you have nothing to worry about and don't need a lawyer, someone who will just drag things out unnecessarily. You can trust the Federation to always find the truth in all matters that come before it. Now, again, did your boss ever criticize your work as a security guard? That's a simple question I'm asking.

Grant: Oh, please, I know what this looks like, but it isn't true!

Interrogator: What isn't true?

Grant: What you're driving at—that I killed Walter Badgett.

Interrogator: Well, did you?

Grant: No, of course not.

Interrogator: But did he ever criticize your work? Again, that's all
I'm asking you.

Grant: Yes, once.

Interrogator: And when was that?

Grant: Last week.

Interrogator: So, then, just before he went missing? Correct?

Grant: Yes, but that doesn't mean I killed him.

Interrogator: We'll see. Now, where did this conversation take
place?

Grant: At his house. He called me to come over to his house to talk
with him.

Interrogator: Why not at the lumberyard? That was your workplace,
wasn't it?

Grant: Yes, but it was raining that day.

Interrogator: Well, what did he say about your work when you went
to his house?

Grant: He said he thought I wasn't really inspecting the lumberyard
as I was supposed to.

Interrogator: And why did he think that?

Grant: He said that when he went to his office in the yard recently
to work on his finances, he found the office door unlocked. And

he thought it looked like material was missing from some of the storage sheds in the yard.

Interrogator: Did he mention any specific material?

Grant: Yes, he thought that some of the plywood sheets and two-by-fours must have been removed. Probably one-by-six planking, too. He said he was sure of that much, but he didn't take an inventory.

Interrogator: Okay, what did he think had happened to his lumber?

Grant: He accused me of selling it to people. But I didn't! I swear I didn't! I never let anyone into that yard. And nobody ever asked me to let them in or to take anything. And I never took anything from the yard, either. Never!

Interrogator: How often did you inspect the lumberyard?

Grant: I was supposed to check it every day at different times but usually at night, since that's when thieves would most likely be around. But I never saw anyone. Not even once.

Interrogator: You say you were supposed to check the yard every day, but did you really check it that often? Did you go inside and check the storage sheds and the office?

Grant: Most times.

Interrogator: What do you mean by "most times"?

Grant: All right, sometimes. What I did most days was walk by the front of the yard along the street and look through the fence. I could see a lot that way, so I didn't always go inside the gate. But I always checked the gate to be sure it was locked."

Interrogator: Just the front gate?

Grant: Well, yes.

Interrogator: But doesn't the lumberyard have a back gate, also?

Grant: Yes.

Interrogator: And did you check that daily?

Grant: No.

Interrogator: Did you ever check it?

Grant: Well …

Interrogator: Well, did you?

Grant: No. Since the front gate was always locked, there didn't seem to be a reason to check the back one. No one went back there.

Interrogator: But our detectives found evidence by the back gate of activity—drag marks. Did you see those?

Grant: No.

Interrogator: So, you didn't go inside the sheds or the office every day as Mr. Badgett instructed you to. And you never inspected the back gate as he no doubt also instructed you to do. And you didn't find obvious signs of activity by the back gate because you never went there, yet our detectives found them right away. Instead of what you were supposed to do, you were only looking through the front gate to inspect the yard in the dark. Is that what you're telling me?

Grant: No, not always at night, sometimes in the day. At different times on different days. Didn't seem to be any real need to look anytime, really. Everything looked okay from what I could see. Nothing ever changed.

Interrogator: But you were supposed to go inside and inspect every day, including inside the storage sheds and the back gate, isn't that right?

Grant: Well, yeah.

Interrogator: But you didn't. Now Mrs. Badgett tells us that her husband found the office building door unlocked. That seems like an obvious thing for you to check. But you would have to have gone inside the yard to do that, now, wouldn't you?

Grant: Sure.

Interrogator: But you didn't go inside. So, Mr. Badgett was right to be upset with you, wouldn't you say?

Grant: Maybe a little, but not blowing a gasket like he did. He could be very mean, you know, he really could. Everybody knew that. He had a reputation for that.

Interrogator: Did it make you mad when he talked to you that way, when he was being "very mean," as you put it?

Grant: Well, sure it did. It would make anybody mad to have someone standing over you, yelling at you, and accusing you of not doing your job and being lazy and all that kind of stuff he said to me.

Interrogator: And that made you mad enough to kill him, didn't it?

Grant: No! Of course not! Now, see! You're trying to trap me again. I'm not that kind of person. Look, I'll admit being a little lax in my job, but I'm not a killer.

Interrogator: But this time you snapped. You did kill him, didn't you? His criticism made you angry, and you knew he was going down there to inspect the lumberyard for himself, and you knew what he'd find. Maybe he would even do some spot inventories, and then you'd be found out for sure. So, you went there, waited for him, and killed him when he arrived. Didn't you?

Grant: No! No, I didn't!

Interrogator: You waited for him at the lumberyard because you knew he wanted to inspect it for himself. You knew when he was coming, so you waited there in one of those big dark storage sheds, and when he showed up, you attacked him, didn't you? No sense denying it now.

Grant: No, no, I didn't even go back to the yard once he bawled me out. I reckoned he was going to check it for himself after that and just cut me out. I had to get busy looking for another job or else I'd end up a vagrant like all the other guys I know.

Interrogator: All the more reason why you killed him, isn't it? He was going to cut off your livelihood, that very mean man.

Grant: But I didn't kill him. I never even saw him again after I left his house the day he talked to me the way he did. It was awful.

Interrogator: Well, let me explain your situation now. There is a judge sitting in the very next room right now, just waiting to hear your case. If you confess, he is likely to be lenient with you and send you to a nice work camp. You'll be there for maybe five years. But if you persist in your lies, then your punishment will be correspondingly harsher, a camp with worse living conditions and harder labor, much harder, and lasting for many years, probably more than ten, maybe even longer than that. I can't tell you that part for certain because it's all up to the judge. Now, knowing what can happen to you, do you still deny killing Walter Badgett?

Grant: But how can the judge hear my case? You have no evidence, no witnesses. Do you even have a corpse? How do we even know that Walter Badgett is dead? Maybe he just went away for a while. Who knows? Or if he is dead, you don't know how he was killed or who could have done it, because I can tell you for sure that it wasn't me. There were a lot of people who didn't like him. That's why I want a lawyer, just like I told you when we started.

Interrogator: Plausibility is our evidence, Citizen Grant, and in your case it looks quite sound. Rock solid, I'd say. The fact that Walter Badgett has disappeared is our corpse. The fact that you argued with him and the fact that he fired you because you weren't doing your job properly—that's the motivation. You have already confessed to that much. Then you got angry and desperately afraid you'd become a vagrant, as you yourself just said. And when you did, you confessed to the motive for the murder. You knew very well that Mr. Badgett was going to the yard to inspect it for himself, since he couldn't trust you to do it properly. His wife heard him tell you that. So, we have a witness. That knowledge provided you with the opportunity to murder Walter Badgett. So, you waited for him there in the lumberyard and killed him. That's why he is missing. We don't need—and the judge doesn't need—more evidence in such an obvious case. And as for the lawyer you keep pestering me for, this country has had a long history, before the Federation came to power, of defense lawyers needlessly confusing and delaying court proceedings—and sometimes even managing to defeat justice. We don't allow that any more. Cases are decided by what makes sense, not by technicalities. And your case will be an easy one for this judge to decide.

Grant: Oh, God, no!

Interrogator: I wouldn't appeal to God if I were you, not in front of a Federation judge. Now, will you sign a confession and make things easier for yourself, or must I recommend the worst to the judge you've kept waiting so long?

Chapter 13: Delia Hodge

By the second week of November the wind had shifted to the northwest and brought with it moisture from the Great Lakes. The temperature plunged from the unseasonably warm sixties at midday to the mid-twenties during the night. Then the moisture in the air salted down as icy snow—not a lot, but enough that by morning it gave unmistakable notice of worse winter days to come.

Foreseeing this overdue change in the weather, Dale and Rodney had availed themselves of the best-fitting and warmest winter coats they could find in the Southside Shelter, plus gloves and scarves and knit hats. They did their "shopping" as soon as the winter gear became available. Rodney's white scarf, although it had been cleaned, was, nevertheless, stained. He thought it was blood-stained, for he had been thinking often of Walter Badgett's blood flowing on the hillside behind the lumberyard and was troubled daily by this and other recollections of the murder. Dale's scarf, a bright red one, had repairs sewn in several spots, and his right glove had a hole at the tip of the forefinger that admitted the cold air.

The night they came to the shelter to search for coats, they stayed and slept there, wondering if they had done the right thing in building the shantyboat now that it was so cold. After all, they were still dependent on the shelter for a place to shower and swap old clothes for washed and repaired ones, just as they were still dependent on the canteen for their food, since they had no money to purchase their own. Plus, checking themselves out after a shower and change of clothes every day in order to return to the shanty would call attention to themselves, even though it would allow two other vagrants who might still be lingering outside the shelter hoping desperately for unexpected vacancies to have cots for the night. Consequently, their use of the shantyboat as a residence remained limited by their need for the Federation's services dispensed through the shelters and canteens.

Nevertheless, the next morning following the first snowfall, a day that dawned sunny but brisk and bitterly cold, they reassured one another over coffee and oatmeal in the canteen that they had been right to pursue even this modicum of personal freedom provided by their shantyboat, that at the very least the shanty gave them shelter against the frosty winter winds during the day. They convinced themselves of this claim all the more since circumstances had forced them to kill for their little piece of freedom and do so not once but twice. Of course, this fact they carefully kept unspoken, even to one another. Nor was there ever any report of the murders on the local news they saw on the nights they did spend in the shelter. But since they were now spending more than half their nights in the shanty, they reasoned that they could easily have simply missed the news coverage.

After leaving the canteen and recovering Rodney's knife from its latest hiding place, they discussed their new status. Specifically, they pondered the differences between their old freedoms during the Happy Times, which they still recalled and cherished, Rodney perhaps more than Dale, and their new dependence on the Federation's version of compassion. This secular charity was intended to shepherd all vagrants through the Greater Depression toward a bright new day of absolute parity for all. All, that is, except the Federation's enemies.

As cold gusts pushed them along Camden Avenue toward the path to the shanty, they heard a voice calling to them just as they were passing the lumberyard entrance. Dale recognized the voice at once, just as a month earlier he had recognized Walter Badgett's. But this voice had a much different effect on him.

"Dale! Dale, is that you?" A young woman's voice called out from the porch of the house across the street from the lumberyard. A vibrato of desperation propelled that voice toward them through the November wind. Both men immediately turned toward the sound only to have the wind glaze their eyes with tears. Even so, they could make out a woman with a long black coat pulled around her figure, standing on the porch and waving to them while the wind tossed her bright red hair about her.

"Delia!" Dale called back to her as he looked in her direction. "Yes, it's me. Are you okay?"

"I guess I am, but can I talk with you—for just a little while?"

"Sure, just a second." Dale turned to Rodney, lowered his voice, and said, "I better go see what she wants. She might know something we need to know. Maybe something about us."

"Then, indeed, you'd better go talk to her. Lucky you from the looks of her!" Rodney said with a smile. "I'll be at the shanty or nearby gathering wood for the stove when you get there … if you get there." Rodney smiled again, more broadly this time.

Ignoring the implications of Rodney's reply, Dale answered, "Yeah, I better go see her, but I will meet you later, don't worry about that."

"Okay, better hurry, though. She sounds concerned."

Rodney turned his back to the wind again and continued up the street toward the path they'd made through a vacant lot that eventually led down to the river and the shantyboat. Dale turned to the west wind and hurried across the street, mounting the steps that led from the sidewalk up to the porch of Delia Hodge's home. She was still waiting for him.

"Hello, Delia. Here I thought your house was empty. Walked by it all summer but never saw anyone."

"Oh, it was empty most of the summer. But let's go inside, out of this cold wind, so we can talk."

Dale held the door open for her as she entered the house. Before following her inside, he looked over his shoulder, across the street, wondering just how far beyond the lumberyard down the hill toward the river Delia could see from her porch as well as wondering *what* she might have seen. But just a quick glance told him that everything beyond the yard's rear gate was obscured by the woods. After his brief surveillance, he followed her inside.

The Hodges lived in a modest house, very much like the others in the neighborhood—two stories, white wooden siding, grey cement steps rising to a full-width front porch, its roof supported by wide square wooden columns and its base framed with white latticework, spattered today with mud from the recent rain that had ended in snow flurries when the wind shifted and the temperature dropped.

Most of these homes had been built at about the same time to accommodate the families of the blue-collar workers who toiled in the numerous factories that had once lined the south side of the river. All of the factories were gone now, lost to changes in taste, technology, and foreign competition. Many of the houses were now as much as one hundred and fifty years old and had been patched and repaired many times over inside and out. And now many more were wanting new attention to keep them livable. A few had simply been abandoned after the onset of the Greater Depression, their owners unable to sustain their mortgages or maintain the houses in livable condition.

Inside the Hodges' home the accommodations were just as modest as the house's exterior but in good condition—a small living room directly inside the front door, walls painted flat white, a narrow staircase to the right of the entrance with an unadorned banister and handrail, both dark brown, the finish nearly worn off by use, and above it all a half-globe glass ceiling light held in place by a tarnished bronze thumbscrew. The demi-globe was clearly yellowed with age even when unlit. After stepping inside, Dale could see a similar one at the top of the stairs. Another room, apparently a study or bedroom, occupied the space to the right of the staircase.

Delia stood in the morning sunlight, which flooded into the living room from the windows on the east side of the house. She had only pulled her black flannel coat around her shoulders, an act obviously done in considerable haste when she saw Dale walking along the street, or at least someone she thought was Dale. Now with her impression confirmed, she stood beside that man, close by, not moving, as he closed the front door behind them. The sunlight fell on her rich red hair which, now untroubled by the wind, spread across the collar and neckline of her black flannel coat. When Dale turned to her after closing the door, they stared at each other momentarily, she with her bluish-grey eyes fixed on his face, a face darkly shadowed even in the morning light for want of a shave. It was a long look they shared after she initiated it, as if to confirm one another's identity after a long separation. Then she spoke again.

"Here, let me take your coat, Dale." She shook off her own and folded it over her left arm. "I'll put it with mine in the closet." Beneath her coat she wore a short green and white striped dress. *More appropriate for warm weather than this bitter blustery cold day*, Dale thought, *but perhaps she has nothing else to wear*. His sympathy for her rose proportionally with this thought.

He hesitated at first to remove his own coat, for he knew that sewn onto its lining was a yellow label with bold black letters stating "SOUTHSIDE COMMUNITY SHELTER." To avoid revealing the source of his coat, which he regarded as shameful evidence of his vagrant-slave status, though Delia could no doubt guess that anyway, he partially turned his back to her while he removed the coat and quickly folded it over his arm to conceal the label. Then he said to her, "Here, let me hold both coats while you hang them up."

"Okay, thanks," she replied, handing him her coat, then stepped close by him, brushing against his arm, to reach the closet near the front door. She pulled back a beige curtain that served as the closet door. The curtain hung by metallic rings from a bronze-colored rod wedged across the top of the doorway, rather like a shower curtain. "There," Delia said with some satisfaction after hanging up the coats and pulling the curtain back in place to conceal the closet's contents. "Now let's sit down and talk." As she spoke to him, she placed a hand on his shoulder to maintain her balance as she kicked off her shoes, simple black flats scuffed along the toes with virtually no heels at all, if they had ever had any. *Maybe, like the dress, she has no other*, Dale wondered. She left the shoes by the closet and padded her way across the carpeted floor barefooted toward a sofa on the far side of the room.

Dale followed her, amazed at the sight of her naked feet and the curvature of her legs, but wondering as he went, *Why did she just do that, kick off her shoes? And what does she know? Did she hear Badgett when he bellowed as Rodney stuck him? She was no doubt at home then. And if she did hear him, she had time to rush to a window or even to go out onto the porch and look. Could have taken a good look. And if she did, she would have recognized Badgett for certain. He would still have been facing her direction if she were fast enough to reach a window or the porch. Or even if he had already fallen at Rodney's feet with his heart stuck through from behind with Rodney's lock-back knife, she would still have recognized him. She wouldn't have known Rodney, though. Doesn't seem to know him now. But if she continued to watch—and who wouldn't have, seeing a murder like that, if that's what she did— then she would have seen me, too. And watched me help Rodney drag Badgett down the hill and out of sight. Maybe she even watched, shocked by the horror of what she was seeing, when I came back to relock the rear gate. And later still when I tried to wash away the blood on the bank with buckets of river water. Then, in those instances, and without a doubt, she would have seen my face and known it was me assisting with Badgett's murder. She could easily have done all that, seen the whole thing. Yet nothing happened. That means if she did see us, she didn't tell, but she could have! Oh, God, what does she know, really?*

The sofa was covered with a soft blue throw made from plush fabric that had worn bare in a few spots. Several additional tufts seemed to be loose, as well. On the wall immediately above the sofa was a painting, or more likely the reproduction of one. Its left border was taken up entirely by the black trunk of a ruined tree, one with rough, craggy bark. Clinging to the tree with dark talons and taking up the bulk of the painting's center-right space was an owl, large and richly colored with reddish brown feathers, flecks and stripes of black, and patches of grey and creamy tan. In her hooked yellow beak she held a limp field mouse, which she offered for shredding to her owlets, three of which protruded from a dark cavity in the tree, stretching their necks toward the mouse and clicking their tiny beaks, or so it seemed, as sight can become sound in the magic of art. The top portion of the painting was a tangle of broken and jagged branches and twigs. Behind them a full moon glowed, backlighting the entire scene. And across the face of that moon soared another owl, more distant, dipping its wings toward the owl on the tree, its large yellow eyes fixed on her.

Delia sat first, positioning herself directly below the owl hen. She crossed her legs, provocatively Dale thought, by lifting her left leg a bit higher than necessary to place it across her right knee, exposing as she did much of her thighs. As Dale sat down beside her, he found that he sank deeper into the sofa's soft seat cushion than he expected.

Seeing the surprise on his face, Delia explained, while laughing lightly and brushing her naked foot against his pantleg, for she didn't seem so desperate any longer, "The sofa belonged to my parents. It's quite old, and I'm afraid it's seen better days. Not so springy any more." She also touched his arm lightly, almost playfully, as she spoke, as though requesting his indulgence.

"That's okay," Dale replied. "By now we've all seen better days. I know I have. But you look as pretty as ever, Delia. You really do." She smiled and seemed to blush. "Besides," he continued, "everybody is trying to make things last as long as they can. And you can't blame them. Replacements are impossible to get, even if you've got money. But, say, where is your little boy? Sammy, isn't that his name?"

81

"I'm up here," a little voice called down the stairs immediately, as if responding to a stage cue.

"Sammy!" Delia said sharply and stamped her bare foot on the carpet loud enough for Sammy to hear. "Go back in your room and shut the door. Read your books like I told you." Promptly, a door upstairs closed.

Dale was impressed that Delia could create such thunder with a foot so small and naked and an ankle so trim. Smiling at Sammy's impertinence, he asked, "How old is he now?"

"Oh, he's old enough to be curious about everything, as you can tell. It's getting harder to control him," she said, recrossing her legs even more carelessly than before. "But to answer your question, age-wise he's four now, nearly five."

"And he can read?"

"Well, he thinks that reading is the same thing as looking at the pictures in books. He only knows a few words so far, but he's eager to learn. I both do and don't look forward to his going to school. It'll be nice to see him have other children to play with every day and begin to learn some social skills instead of just being with me all day every day. But the schools have become so poor for academic learning, even worse than when you and I attended. All they teach the kids now is how to obey the Federation's rules and regulations and how to spy on others who might not be obeying those rules. And by 'others,' the Federation means people like other children and even the children's own parents. But not their teachers, of course. No time for math or science or spelling or anything else they actually need to be learning, but plenty of time for politics. Good thing no one spies on that. No, just learn to obey; that's all that counts. That's the goal of learning now—learn to conform and learn to spy. That's all you need to know. As a parent, you send the school innocent little kids, and the school sends you back little espionage agents. That's what I hear from all the parents in the neighborhood who have kids in school already. Nothing good, Dale, nothing at all."

"Yeah, I've heard the same thing. Doesn't seem like there's much you can do about it, though. All the private and religious schools were closed a long time ago, when we were still small. My kids hadn't started school yet when I last saw them, so, like you, I'm going on hearsay about the current state of things."

"What do you mean 'when you last saw them'? What happened to them?"

"They're gone. Their mother took them and left me after the lumberyard layoffs."

"Where did she go?"

"I don't really know. She left with another man, someone I guess she thought could take better care of her and the kids than I could. As it turns out, she was no doubt right. Soon, I lost the house and everything in it as well as her and the kids."

"Gone! Just like that, you mean?" Delia snapped her fingers.

"Yes, just like that. One day while I was out looking for work. About nine months ago now. When I came home, they weren't there. Clothes and toys and such gone, too. As much as they could gather up, it seemed like. A neighbor woman told me she saw them leave. A man with a large white car drove up, she said, and loaded their things into it. They all got in and drove away. Not even a note left behind. Just gone. But must have been someone with connections to still have a car he could use when he wanted."

"That's terrible, Dale!" Delia said with as much conviction as she could muster while recrossing her legs once again and watching Dale watch her do it. "I could never do anything like that myself."

"I guess not, but on the porch you sounded worried about something—something other than Sammy, I'm guessing."

"Yes, you're right, I am very worried. It's Randy. After you all got laid off last year, Randy took off for Pittsburgh to find work."

"Yes, I remember his saying that's what he'd do. Thought he'd have a better chance there."

"Well, he did all right. He found a job working in a steel warehouse driving a forklift, much like his work here in the lumberyard. They're busy supplying materials for all the shelters and canteens that the government is building around the country. Randy's company has several federal contracts, Randy said."

"Well, good for him. Are you moving up to Pittsburgh, then, to be with him?"

"No, we're not. But Sammy and I went to join him for most of the summer. He has just a little efficiency-type apartment; that's all he could afford right now. So, it was cramped with the three of us and not much fun for Sammy and me being in a strange place and Randy at work all the time. Seems that since the use of lumber has been banned for new construction, demand for steel buildings and steel construction materials has shot way up. And, as I said, the warehouse where Randy works stores and ships those kinds of materials. They have so much business right now, what with the federal contracts, that Randy works lots of overtime. Let me tell you, Sammy and I went through an entire library of picture books this summer while Randy was at work!"

"That sounds great. And it explains why I didn't see anyone here at your house during the summer when I walked by. So, I thought the house was vacant now. Sure wish I could find work somewhere around here the way Randy did in Pittsburgh."

"Yes, it was a big relief to have money coming in again. At least, it was while I had it."

"Was? Did something happen?"

"Well, once he landed the warehouse job, Randy started sending me money each month to cover our expenses here." Delia's voice sounded distracted now, as though the thoughts were coming to her from a great distance and passing through a barrier of some kind. She was staring at the carpet in front of her bare feet.

"Sent?" Dale asked, leaning toward her. "Isn't he still sending you money?"

Delia looked up briefly, then lowered her head now as she spoke and started wringing her hands in her lap. "No. No, he's not," she replied, weeping now, "and I haven't heard from him, either. I've called his workplace and his apartment building. Left him messages repeatedly, probably ten different times by now. But he hasn't returned any of my calls. I don't know what's happened to him." Then, looking up, she said, "Oh, Dale, I don't know what to do!" She leaned toward him now, and he put his arm around her shoulders as she cried softly against his chest.

"We fought all summer," she continued, raising her head again, and whispering now into Dale's left ear, presumably to ensure that Sammy did not hear her desperation. "Fought mostly about this house. He wanted me to go back and sell it and move up there, but I didn't want to. I told him it wasn't worth doing. You can only give houses away right now, since nobody has the money to buy one, even though many people really need them. 'Fine,' he said, 'then just leave it. What's another empty house? They're all over the place.' That was his feeling. But I couldn't bring myself to do that.

84

Now I'm afraid he's abandoned me and Sammy. That's why I had to talk to you, Dale."

"You haven't heard from him at all?"

"No, not a word for over a month now, and I'm running out of money. Soon I'll have to sign up for assistance so we can eat in the Women and Children's Canteen, but it's so far away. We'll end up having to take a bus just to go back and forth to get our meals. And bad weather is already starting. But more than that, I'll soon have no money to pay for utilities—so no heat or water or electricity. When those are gone, we'll have to move into one of those shelters for homeless families, and this house will be quickly lost to squatters, you can bet on that."

"I don't think they'll let you into one of those permanent family shelters unless you have a notice of eviction," Dale cautioned her. "That's what I've heard, at least. My friend Rodney seems to know more about those things than I do. Otherwise, according to him, you can only use the overnight shelters the way Rodney and I have to do. So, you would still need a place to go during the day—a place that's safe. Otherwise, the two of you will be on the street with microchips fastened behind your earlobes like the rest of us vagrants—with no place to go and nothing to do except try to escape the weather. Also, do you still have a mortgage? Is a bank involved?"

"Yes, we have a small mortgage. My parents helped us get this house, so it's not a big mortgage."

"Well, the bank or mortgage company might give you an eviction notice to use if you just tell them your situation—that is to say, that you can't keep up the mortgage payments and will soon have to give up the house anyway."

"But again, that's just giving the house away and losing all the equity we've paid into it plus the money my parents gave us for the down payment when we got married. I don't want to do that. I won't do that! This house is the only savings Randy and I have and the only security we have against poverty, against spending the winter on the streets. Somehow, I have to hold onto it! If there were only some way I could keep paying for the utilities and buying our own food! That's all Sammy and I really need—a source of income. It doesn't have to be a lot. And I certainly don't want to have Sammy suffer! Oh, there's so much to worry about, Dale!" She was weeping again and leaning on him.

"Can your parents help you? Maybe you can live with them."

"Maybe. I haven't asked them yet. And don't really want to. I'm ashamed to, really. That'll be my last resort. They're living on a government pension themselves, and like most other people, they just barely make ends meet. Instead of asking them, I was thinking of asking Walter for help first—Walter Badgett, I mean. He'd always been so nice to me. But ..."

Dale stiffened. Responding haltingly, he interrupted what Delia was about to say with, "Well ... Well, do you really think he would help you? That is, have you been in touch with him lately?"

"No, not lately. Haven't you heard? He's gone missing and may have been killed." She sat upright now, alert and no longer weeping. "In fact, the police were here just last week, or maybe it was two weeks ago."

"You mean, here at your house?" Dale couldn't contain his concern now.

"No, no, not here. I mean, across the street, at the lumberyard. They were there for quite a while searching for clues about Walter's disappearance, I guess. I saw Mrs. Badgett with them, too. She shouted at them quite a few times. You know how she is. She was complaining about what a poor job she thought they were doing and kept telling them to look here and look there as though she were the police commissioner in charge of the whole investigation. I didn't talk to any of them. Actually, I was surprised they *didn't* come over here to ask if I had seen anything, since our house is so close."

"Well, *did* you see anything?"

"No, but Mrs. Badgett pointed at our house several times as though she wanted them to check with me, but they never did. Finally, all of them ended up down by the rear gate as though they'd found something there."

Dale could feel himself stiffen even more now, tensing with fear. "What did they find?"

"I'm not sure, but from what I could hear, it sounded as though Agnes made them go down toward the river."

"But you say they never talked to you and you never saw anything?"

"No. Then later, I heard a report on one of the ghost radio stations that have started up in the area that the guard Walter had hired to check on the yard was arrested and charged with Walter's murder."

"Murder? They found Badgett's body?"

"No, at least not that I know of, but I guess whatever they did find during their search made them think that Walter had been murdered and that the guard was guilty of doing it. The news report mentioned a quarrel Walter had with the guard about his work. That happened the day before Walter's disappearance. In fact, it's the same guard Walter had watching out for my house while I was in Pittsburgh. His name is Ellis, if I remember correctly, Ellis Grant."

"And the police arrested this Grant guy, you say, this guard?"

"Yes, according to the radio reports, they did. In fact, he's already been tried, convicted, and sent away. Off to one of the labor camps for the rest of his life, I suppose. All that even though Walter's body was never found. I've been wondering what his wife will do with the lumberyard if Walter really is dead."

"And this same guard watched your house, the same guard who supposedly killed Badgett?" Dale asked again, having trouble controlling his curiosity and incredulity.

"Yes, I guess the same one. I only met him twice, once before I left and once when I came back."

"How did that work out—his watching the house, I mean? Any problems with the house or the lumberyard when you came back?"

"No, none with the house. I don't know about the lumberyard, but then I suppose both of them being on a main street like Camden helps some to keep away trouble. I did hear there were abandoned houses on the side streets nearby here that were vandalized during the summer, so there is plenty of danger about. And—this is what really frightens me, Dale—during the winter, squatters have become a serious problem, as you probably know. Not only that, but they've also gotten bolder and bolder. I've already had someone try to break in here at night since it turned colder, just a few days ago, in fact. And a person can't even have a gun any more to protect himself, not even a woman. Not that I would have one in the house with a little child, but still! Oh, Dale, how did it all get like this—everything so mixed up and falling apart?" She was crying and pressing against his chest again.

"Seems like that's a long, twisted story, Delia." He had both arms around her now and was thankful that he had spent the night in the shelter, because he took a shower and changed into fresh clothes. "It's all too complicated for me to understand, but again, my buddy, Rodney, seems to. He's pretty smart about such things. But I know just what you mean about how scary it is. I lost everything myself after the layoff, and I do mean everything. Even my wife and kids, as I said. So, my feelings about Walter Badgett aren't as kind as yours."

Delia sat erect now, then leaned forward a bit to stare into Dale's face. "Rodney? Is that the same person you mentioned before? Is that the fellow you were walking with when I called to you this morning?"

"Yes. I met him earlier this summer, downtown, or what people still call downtown, the area near the courthouse. We've been palling around since then. Trying to look out for each other, you might say. You really need someone to watch your back these days when you're out on the streets or even in the shelters and canteens."

"I thought I'd seen the two of you go by here together, but I wasn't sure it was you or the same person with you that I was seeing this morning, all bundled up in your coats. But today I thought I'd take a chance. I'm so glad it was you."

Chapter 14: Delia's Plan

Delia squirmed a bit on the couch beside Dale, apparently a bit unsure about what to say next. "I'm glad I did stop you, because I have something else I want to say … or rather, ask you. But it's something positive this time. At least, I think it is. Not just pouring out my own troubles on you, since I can see you have plenty of your own."

"Okay, what else is there? I'm glad to listen and help if I can." Despite his words, Dale was a bit apprehensive about Delia's change to the more matter-of-fact tone she'd used when relating the story of the guard. But Dale was, nevertheless, completely enraptured by the intimacy of the embrace he had shared with Delia during her pleading and the degree to which the skirt of her dress kept rising during their conversation, especially now as she uncrossed and recrossed her legs again, probably from anxiety, he was thinking.

"I need your help, Dale," she began. "I really do." She was now on the edge of the sofa cushion and turned almost completely toward him. "Since I haven't heard from Randy, I'm getting desperate, as I was telling you. While he was gone, Walter helped me some, both before I went to Pittsburgh and after I returned."

"You mean, help in addition to the guard?"

"Yes, much more than the guard. Walter gave me money. I'm sure you know he was always after me. Everyone could see that. He flirted with me all the time, shamelessly, even with Randy standing right next to us. Walter even put his arm around my waist a time or two, in a joking way, of course. He'd always find some excuse to touch me, if only on the arm or the shoulder. I guess he knew he had the upper hand with Randy and me, as he did with most people, and didn't mind if he took advantage of me with these little intimacies. He didn't seem to mind at all if he hurt Randy's feelings while he was at it. Probably was even doing it on purpose just to show he could get away with it. He was the boss, after all, and could do pretty much whatever he wanted. But it really did hurt Randy to watch him do that. He would just burn with hatred afterward and sometimes would take it out on me, verbally at least, since he didn't dare attack Walter. Sometimes, Randy would claim that I was flirting back, leading Walter on to get favors from him."

"Actually, I can just see Badgett acting like that. I know he was always looking at you when you came across the street to visit Randy at lunchtime. To be honest about it, though, all of us guys enjoyed seeing you. We were all jealous of Randy having such a pretty wife."

"Really, is that true?" Delia seemed to blush. "Guess I was only worried about Walter's advances making Randy so upset."

"Well, I'll admit it's true. We all looked at you when we could," Dale laughed. "But back to Badgett, it did seem like he was always used to getting what he wanted with everything, as though the world owed him anything he wanted."

"That's right. And his wife, Agnes, if you know her, is even worse. After a while I could just feel Walter's eyes on me as he stood at that window in the corner of his little office. I could feel it every time I went over there. But what could I do? We needed the wages he paid Randy."

"I understand, but what is it you were going to ask me? What is the 'something else' you mentioned? What kind of help do you need that I can give you? You know I don't have any money."

"No, I'm certainly not asking you for money, but I have an idea how we can get money—an idea I think can help us all—you, me, and Sammy, even your friend, Rodney, if he's willing. And others around here, especially some of my neighbors." Excitement came to Delia's voice now, and she moved close enough to Dale that her right leg touched his left.

"I know I said I was desperate before," Delia continued, "but being desperate has given me an idea, a plan for getting out of these troubles."

"Wow, that does sound interesting." He wanted her to lean toward him again. He wanted even more to touch her leg, but her mood seemed to have changed now from flirtation to business. "What is it? Come on, tell me about your plan." He leaned toward her this time, playfully.

"Well, when I got back here from Pittsburgh, I went around the neighborhood to catch up on what had happened during the summer, since there so little news these days and even less you can actually trust. There's more reliable news on the few pirate radio stations that have popped up than on the Federation's TV channels. Well, anyway, it turns out that a lot of the women around town are alone, just as I am right now, because their husbands have gone off to work somewhere else, or at least to look for work, and are sending money back home when they can. A few other women have lost their husbands to the work camps for one reason or another and live entirely on Federation assistance. But a few of them are still managing to live in their homes, or at least trying to. All these wives complain that there is no one to do the little chores around the house any more, like fixing a running toilet or a dripping faucet or caulking drafty windows. Little stuff like that, things their husbands used to do. And the businesses that used to do those kinds of things—the plumbers and electricians and HVAC businesses—those services have mostly closed up, because the business taxes got so high they couldn't continue to operate or couldn't get enough skilled tradesmen to do the work, even though people still needed them.

"I know women and older people around here would be willing to pay to have these little jobs done for them, even if they had to miss a meal or two to do it. They are all dreadfully afraid that something serious will happen that will jeopardize their homes. I asked them about the kinds of problems they were having. Soon, I began to develop an idea about how to help them. Some of them already have long lists of things someone could easily take care of, most in a single day. Yet these are problems that seem threatening to them. So, that's when I thought of you and remembered seeing you walk up and down Camden. I remembered that you used to be a handyman before you came to work in the lumberyard. Randy told me that. It is true, isn't it?"

"Yep, sure is. Supported my family that way for about five years before I got the steadier work in the lumberyard."

"Well, when I started seeing you and your friend walking by the house after I got back, I began to think that maybe you could do that kind of work for these people. In fact, I think you would have enough work just on this side of town to keep both you and Rodney busy all winter at the very least, probably much longer."

"You really think so? I'd given up on handyman work, I have to tell you. Too much trouble for too little reward when I was doing it. Had to have Federation approval for nearly everything you could think of and had to pay fees to get it."

"I'm nearly positive it would be worth your while now because things have changed so much. And we'd do it in a way that we wouldn't pay the Federation anything, not a single dollar. Demand for that kind of work is sky-high right now, and people to do it are few and far between. And I'm saying that based on just the people I've talked to. I believe if we encouraged the ones I know about to tell others how you came and fixed their problems, there would be no telling how much more business we could have. And pretty fast, I think."

"You keep saying 'we.' How do you see yourself fitting into this?"

"We could use this house as our headquarters. I still have a telephone. People would call here to request repairs, then I would schedule them for you guys. I would be your dispatcher and scheduler, I guess you'd call it. And your bookkeeper, too. I was a bookkeeper, after all, and an auditor for one of the local banks before I married Randy. Not only that, but I also did some part-time bookkeeping afterward, even after Sammy was born. For example, I helped Walter with his accounts quite a few times. He had no head for money, not really, but didn't like to admit it, especially not to Agnes. If it hadn't been for the money Agnes brought to their marriage—her parents had the town's biggest dry cleaning business—he would never have been able to open the lumberyard. He would keep making little mistakes here and there in the yard's financial accounts and then couldn't find the mistakes later. He'd get frustrated with himself, especially because he didn't want Agnes to find out. She's always been a stickler over every little detail. So, then Walter would call me to come over to help him get his books straightened out before Agnes discovered his mistakes and started nagging him about them. But then Walter would use those occasions to start flirting with me again, and Randy would get jealous again, especially if I couldn't come back right away, even though I was bringing in some badly needed money for us."

"But how would we travel to these jobs? They could be anywhere, couldn't they? Suppose we got calls for places that the bus lines don't service? How would Rodney and I get there to do the work?"

"Ah, I don't think you'll need the buses at all. Besides, they'd waste too much of your valuable time. There's a retired fellow just up the street from here—Cal Burdette. I've known Cal for a little while now. Nice old guy. He used to have a local delivery service and recently retired, fed up just like you were over all the regulations. But he still has the panel truck he used for the business. He's afraid the Federation will eventually want to confiscate it if it's not being used for business purposes any more, and if they do, they won't reimburse him for it as they did when they first started eliminating private vehicles. He'd be willing to rent it out to us at a fair price just to keep from losing it. I've already talked to him about that possibility."

"Well, that would be great! A panel truck is perfect for repair work. I used to have one. Keeps the tools and materials out of sight so they don't get stolen yet still has lots of room to haul spare parts. You can even do some repairs inside them in bad weather. I've done that more than a time or two. But one thing—what kind of powertrain does it have? Not one of those all electrics, is it?"

"No, Cal said it's a hybrid, so never has to be charged up from the grid. We all know what a disaster electric vehicles have become."

"That's why I asked."

"As well you should, since now that cold weather is here, you can only charge up an electric vehicle during the midday hours, and sometimes not even then, since the power grid can't always support it, even at night, because people are trying to heat their homes. And midday charging would interfere with your doing repairs."

"Agreed. And one more thing, Delia, just how do you see us working this out—you, me, Rodney, and this Cal Burdette? How would we handle the money?"

"Well, I think I can talk Cal into a day-by-day usage fee, since no doubt there might be at least some days, especially at first, when we wouldn't have any work. He'd be happy with that arrangement, I think. He'd be making a little money from the truck while still having it for personal use on the weekends. Of course, we'd have to pay for the fuel and maintenance. So, that would take care of him. Then all of us—you, me, and Rodney—could split the remaining profits. That would allow me to keep the house and pay for my utilities, to say nothing of buying food. Most of all, it would keep Sammy and me from going to one of the Family Shelters. And you two guys would have work again and money of your own. Is Rodney handy with repair work?"

"Yeah, handy enough. He used to run a junkyard on the north side of town, and in the Navy he managed the engine room on a destroyer. So, he's stripped parts from all kinds of cars and appliances and other machines. Knows plumbing real well, too, from his time in the Navy. And I think he's a pretty fair carpenter." Dale grew cautious again about just how much to tell Delia.

"Good." Delia was leaning close to Dale again, her face almost in his and smiling but no longer whispering. "But I doubt if either of you still has a bank account, do you?"

"No, for sure, mine was gone long ago, gobbled up by the Feds when I lost the house. I think the same's true for Rodney. Why?"

"Because you'll need one to get paid, what with digital currency in use now universally. No cash allowed, unfortunately. Digital makes everything fast and easy but also allows the government to track everyone's financial transactions—everyone's, everywhere, all the time. If they decide to, that is, and track not just those doing something the government or the banks they sponsor think might be illegal, but anyone."

"Yes, Rodney has mentioned that to me before. He says digital currency was a scam right from the start, that the Federation just wanted to convert to it so they could ban cash transactions and confiscate bank accounts easier, do it without people even knowing their money is gone until it's too late for them to do anything about it."

"Well, Rodney is mostly right. At the bank where I worked, I saw that happen to some of our customers. But most of all, I think the Federation wants to be able to identify and shut down any black market sales or any other economic activity that it doesn't already control or approve of, especially activity of any political opponents or other dissenters who may still be around."

"So, how do we get around that problem?"

"Actually, it's rather easy. I made sure I had my own bank account when Randy left so he could deposit money into it for Sammy and me. And as I said, even before I became a self-employed bookkeeper, I was a full-time accounts auditor for one of the local banks, so I'm very familiar with what goes on in banking and government surveillance of bank accounts. As a bank auditor, I saw the Federation confiscating people's savings accounts for various reasons, whether it was their political views or their unwanted economic activity, even legal activity—like the auto dealerships when the Federation wanted to close those down. The government would simply direct the banks to stop giving the auto dealers loans, and then when the dealerships started to fail because they couldn't buy cars to sell, the Federation officials would step in and seize the dealerships' business assets, claiming the dealership had become a liability to the state-run banks. Some of those poor owners of those dealerships went from being fairly wealthy people to paupers in no time at all. Then, eventually, cars were banned anyway.

"But now—and this part is surprising—the Federation actually wants to allow some black market activities to operate as a relief valve for their failing economics. At least, it seems that way. Otherwise, the Federation's economic failures will become obvious to everyone and the negative consequences too great for the Federation to sustain any longer. The top Federation officials are beginning to fear riots, especially over property and bank confiscations and food shortages.

"The type of incidental repair work we'd be doing would be a good example of the smaller discomforts people are experiencing— too small dollar-wise for the Feds to worry about while addressing the kind of annoying problems that can fester and eventually contribute to the political dissent the government does worry about.

"Also, one of the qualities of the Federation workers you can pretty much rely on is that they are lazy. Since for the most part they can't be fired, they take their jobs for granted. If something requires a lot of effort—such as tracking small account transactions—they simply won't do it, not even when they have all the computer power in the world at their disposal, as they do. Now, if I can audit a bank's records, I hope you can see that I have the experience to take care of hiding transactions for a little service operation such as we'll be operating."

"Yes, it sounds like you can. But let me, the simple handyman, try to understand this. What you're saying means our customers would have to do what in order to pay us?"

"They would send you their payment information to the phone I'll provide you with, from their phone to yours. You would check it to be sure it's correct and then forward it to me, again by phone, and I'd deposit it at once, since small deposits tend to be ignored, while large ones are much more likely to draw attention from bank auditors. And Federation auditors regard lots of little deposits as way too much work to follow up on, even if the banks report them. For that reason it's better for us to make a lot of small deposits during the course of the day than to establish a pattern of making one large deposit at the end of each day."

"And how would Rodney and I get paid if cash is out of the question?"

"I would then pay you and Rodney in-kind, at least to begin with, since you don't have electronic accounts of your own any more to receive deposits."

"What does in-kind mean?"

"It means I would pay you with food or clothes or whatever else you might need at the time—all of which I would buy with the proceeds from the work you complete. Again, these payments would be in the form of small transaction that wouldn't catch the attention of an auditor. It is still possible for you to get new bank accounts, of course, but you would almost certainly lose your shelter and canteen benefits. And if my plan doesn't work for some reason, you would still need those, so it's probably wise to wait a bit to open new bank accounts. You might ask Rodney about that, since he seems to be up-to-date on Federation welfare regulations. He probably knows more about those than I do."

"Oh, he's made himself an expert on them, for sure."

"But once we build the business to a reliable income level, then we can talk about getting you guys your own accounts. Actually, by that time we'll need to do that anyway in order to keep all the accounts relatively small. We'll need to spread the money as thin as possible and make payments in-kind as often as possible in order to keep our operation inconspicuous."

"Isn't that what used to be called money laundering when the old mafia families did it?"

"Yes, the very same thing. Those guys weren't stupid, after all. And politicians copied them by laundering their bribery money."

"And would you buy the fuel for the panel truck and the repair parts and other materials we'd need for the repairs, maybe some tools, too?"

"I would. Again, all in small transactions."

"But since the Federation can track all these payments and purchases, wouldn't they get suspicious after a while about someone who's living all alone making all these purchases for her own household?"

"Maybe, but they don't know I'm alone yet. I haven't reported Randy as a deadbeat dad, not yet, at least. If this plan works, I won't report him at all. And just because the Feds can track something doesn't mean they do it. That job's too big even for the Federation, so they have computers that scan transactions for them using algorithms to detect what they regard as unusual activities. And they train the computers to focus only on those activities that go past a certain threshold. Only when those red flags rise do they bother to investigate. Right now that threshold per transaction is two thousand dollars in suspicious activity. They just assume that everything else is either okay, no matter how many transactions are involved, or at least not worth the bother."

"And how do we keep them assuming that?"

"Again, that's easy. We keep track of our purchases and the revenues versus the Federation threshold. When either category gets too close to the two-thousand-dollar mark, we switch to payment in-kind, leaving the transaction algorithms nothing to trace. In the case of repair supplies, we'll have the customers pay for their parts directly as often as possible and then only pay us for the labor. That helps keep our deposits smaller, also. One advantage of the digital money is that the customers can easily make those purchases, even using their phones to do it. No need to actually visit the store itself as long as you know what you need. Plus, there's nothing suspicious about a transaction for a small hardware item, and it's too small dollar-wise for the Federation officials to worry about. As for you and Rodney, you'll have to be paid in-kind anyway. So, nothing to trace there, either. As I said, it's simple as long as we keep close track of what we're doing and be careful, all of which we should do anyway. And that will be mostly my job."

Now Delia seemed anything but distraught. On the contrary, she was confident, even masterful. "Well, Dale, what do you think of my plan?" she asked.

"I'm really excited about this, I really am! You've thought things through completely as far as I can tell. I would never have known all this, especially the banking and thresholds and all that," he said while placing his hand in the middle of her back with a congratulatory pat. "I think this could really work, just like you said. How did you come to think of all this, anyway?"

"Desperation, as I mentioned before, is a great motivator. I began to see that I'd have to do something and do it soon, or else Sammy and I would be out on the streets, and that's not going to happen to us. No matter what I have to do, I won't let that happen."

"But are you sure about our using your house as a headquarters and your phone as the main one we use? That's a lot to put on you. And what if Randy suddenly turns up?"

"Yes, I'm sure about the house and the phone, because we need a headquarters and a business number, and I know how to keep those hidden from Federation scrutiny. As for Randy, I don't think he'll show up now, but if he does, I'll deal with him. In the meantime, we all have to survive, so I can't depend on him any more. Besides, there's one last thing I want to ask you. And you may think I'm being way too forward about this part, but I'll ask it anyway: I'd like you to stay here, stay with me and Sammy."

"You mean move in?"

"Yes, move in. The vagrant who tried to break in at the back door last week really scared me and absolutely terrified Sammy. I scared the guy off by pretending that I was calling for my husband to come downstairs and confront him. I yelled out as though Randy were still in the house. Then I made noises on the steps loud enough to make the vagrant think someone was actually hurrying down the stairs. He ran off after that, but the next squatter might not. This is a dangerous world, as you probably know better than I do. I can keep accounting books just fine, but without a weapon I can't fight off squatters and robbers, and you know very well yourself, Dale, that there's no police protection any more, at least none that amounts to anything, so you can't rely on them for help."

"True enough."

Then they heard the sound of a door opening. Sammy was at the top of the stairs.

"Mom, I'm tired of reading books. When are we gonna eat?"

Delia looked at her wristwatch. "Oops, you're right, honey," she called back to him. "It's lunchtime right now. Come on down here and meet Mr. Nutter before he has to leave."

Sammy toddled down the stairs noisily, disregarding the handrail as he went. He was dressed in blue jeans that barely reached his ankles, exposing dark blue woolen socks, worn without shoes, and a long-sleeved blue sweatshirt with a white block letter "S" on the front. Reaching his mother, he clung shyly to her leg, for she was standing now, before saying, "Hello, Mr. Nutter." He spoke in a shy whisper.

Smoothing Sammy's long red hair with her left hand, Delia turned to Dale and asked, "Would you like to stay and have lunch with us? Hot vegetable soup, homemade, plus ham sandwiches. You're welcome to stay. I have more than enough food."

"Hard to resist that, Delia," Dale replied after shaking Sammy's hand. "Sure beats another serving of watery cabbage soup at the canteen."

"Well, if we can make a deal, you can have lots of meals here. Perhaps Rodney could join us sometimes, too, to give him a break from canteen food. In fact, how about breakfast tomorrow morning, say 7 o'clock, assuming we have a deal? We're always up by then, and I know of at least three repairs close by that I can schedule for you tomorrow morning. Plus, you guys would need to come here anyway to pick up the panel truck and the appointments list. With any luck, I may have some more appointments for you by that time."

"I'll definitely tell him. I'm sure Rodney would appreciate a real breakfast again."

"Oh, one more little enticement," she added with a smile. "There's a lot of different vegetables in my soup but no cabbage."

———◦———

When Dale finally rose from the kitchen table to leave and Sammy was occupied again in his room, this time with a jigsaw puzzle, Delia walked him to the door, clinging to his arm. She had a ham sandwich slathered with mustard and wrapped in wax paper for Dale to give to Rodney. Now she spoke to Dale softly, almost in a whisper, "If you do decide to stay with us, Dale, it doesn't have to lead to anything romantic, not if you don't want it to. You could sleep on the sofa down here in the living room." She pointed to it casually, then added, "Even if that's what you decide, I'll still treat you better than a guard dog. And maybe we could also find Rodney a place close by. Those options are surely a lot better than a random cot in the shelter, aren't they?"

"You're right about that," he replied.

"I thought you'd like living in a house again and having regular meals. It would make communicating about work a lot easier, too."

"That's for sure. In fact, I think you're right all the way around with this whole repair service idea," Dale replied in his own subdued tone. "But if I do stay with you—and I hate to bring this up—what about Randy?"

"Randy again! Never mind him. I told you that already." Then in a softer voice with the irritation drained from it, she added, "At least think about my plan, including the staying here part. Do it for my sake. Please." Then she kissed him on the cheek. "You know, once you and Rodney start working and visiting homes, who knows, he might find a nice woman and a place where he'd be welcomed and appreciated, too. Then he could leave wherever it is you guys are staying now—when you two are not using the shelter, that is. The place you haven't told me about."

Dale ignored her indirect inquiry about the shantyboat and said simply, "Okay, sure, I'll mention that to him." Then he returned her kiss. "But right now I need to go break this news to him about the job offer and get him on board with it. He's got to be wondering what's happened to me by now."

"By the way, what is Rodney's last name? I don't think you ever mentioned it."

"His last name is Tanner. He's Rodney Tanner."

"And is he staying somewhere close by? Where do you two go when you're not at the shelter or canteen? I see you walking by quite a bit, going back and forth. Is it going to be inconvenient for you to get here tomorrow?"

Dale hesitated a moment, thinking of the best possible response. Finally, he said, "It's better, Delia, if you don't know right now. Safer that way in case somebody in authority should ever question you about us. Let's just say we've had to do some things we wouldn't normally do in order to survive on the streets and have a little privacy and safety for ourselves. Let's let it go at that for now. Okay?"

"Okay," she said, raising her hands defensively, "I won't ask about it any more, but you stop worrying about Randy, even though I know you will. That's my job." She seemed absolutely resolute on this matter. Then, before he could open the front door, she added

100

while clutching his arm again at the bicep, "You will come back later today, won't you—to let me know where we stand? I don't like suspense. Plus, I have to call the people on my list to let them know whether or not you'll be coming tomorrow."

"Yes, for sure I'll be back. Just give me a chance to talk with Rodney." Then he kissed her on the cheek again, and they both smiled. "And thanks again for lunch," he said, looking back at her as he stepped onto her windy porch.

"Here," she said, reaching out to him. "Don't forget Rodney's sandwich. He needs a lunch, too."

Chapter 15: Rodney's Turn

The cold west wind pushed Dale up Camden Avenue as he walked toward the shanty with the ham sandwich stashed in his coat pocket. Despite the discomfort of the wind, he thought in amazement about what had happened in the space of a mere half day: Delia reappearing and calling to him; Delia frightened and crying; Delia coquettish, sexy, and inviting; Delia leaving no doubt about her intentions toward him, even though he was a penniless vagrant; and at the end, Delia planning and proposing, perhaps even scheming—he couldn't be sure—but definitely confident and controlling, with a plan of her own for success.

She had developed this elaborate but realistic plan and had done it alone, motivated, as she said, by her desperation. A plan, it seemed to him, with the potential to turn his life around as well as Rodney's and at the same time salvaging what remained of hers. He could see that happening if both he and Rodney would just agree to its terms. It was something that could make their lives worthwhile again. Something potentially with a future and more than a shantyboat to work for and live for. Given everything else that had happened to them, Delia's plan seemed impossibly good, nearly unreal, in fact, especially when compared to the world around them. It could even be for all of them a path back to the time before the Greater Depression. And all this Delia had revealed to him in the space of just a few hours that morning.

When Dale arrived at the shanty, there was a stack of firewood trimmed into nearly equal lengths and neatly piled on the deck by the cabin door. *Typical of Rodney's work*, he thought. *He'll make a good handyman, if only he's willing.* Rodney himself was visible inside the cabin stoking Walter Badgett's antique stove.

"So, here you are at last," Rodney said, looking up from his work and smiling as Dale opened the door. "I was beginning to think you'd given up on shantyboat life for something better."

As Dale entered, the cabin's warm air rushed out, and the fire in the stove nearly went with it until Rodney, with a quick move, closed the firebox door. "Yes, I was beginning to think you had moved in with her. What's her name again?"

"Delia, Delia Hodge. No, at least not yet."

"Not yet! Are you kidding? What does 'not yet' mean?"

"I'll come to that part, but she invited me to stay for lunch, so I did. Fresh vegetable soup and ham sandwiches. And, hey, just look, she sent you this." Dale withdrew the ham sandwich from his coat. "Hope you like mustard."

"She has enough food for you as well as for her son and herself … and me?" Rodney asked, incredulous but taking the sandwich eagerly. "And, yes, I do like mustard. These days I like almost anything to eat that's not canteen cabbage soup, but I really do like mustard."

"And to answer your question, yes, she does have enough food … at least for now. In fact, she wants you to come for breakfast tomorrow, at 7:00, so she can meet you. And just listen to this. She got the fresh vegetables she used for the soup she made from a neighbor woman. And that woman claims she got them from a farmers' market that started up late this summer over on Blizzard Drive."

"Really! Wonder how the farmers around here managed to do that?"

"The woman told Delia that it works like the speakeasies used to way back when."

"Yes, a very long time ago that would be—more than a hundred years—during the last Great Depression."

"Well, just like in those days, you have to know somebody who will tell you the current password, because they're afraid of informers. But once you manage to get inside, according to this neighbor of Delia's, you find a large area of fruit and vegetable stands organized on a dirt floor under a clear plexiglass roof that lets the sunlight in. This woman claims it looks just like the old fruit and vegetable roadside stands that used to be all over this area in the summers, except this one is out of sight from the Feds and works year-round. I'm guessing in the winter they have produce grown in greenhouses somewhere."

"No kidding? I'll bet the Federation will be quick to shut that place down if they do discover it. No private enterprise allowed, you know, with or without a password."

"Well, that brings me to what Delia wanted to talk about."

Rodney opened the door to the stove's firebox again and inserted another log before sitting down on his bunk to unwrap the sandwich and lean back against the window frame. "Well, let me hear about it," he said as he took his first bite of the sandwich.

After removing his hat and coat and seating himself on the edge of his own bunk, Dale began to relate the story of Delia's plight, her fears, and her proposal, omitting only the romantic implications of their morning together, which Rodney seemed to understand anyway and acknowledge with knowing smiles at just the right moments as Dale spoke, filling in for himself the meaning of Dale's pauses and stammers and blushes.

"That's why she's invited you to breakfast tomorrow, to meet her new business partner—that is, if you agree to her plan."

"And if I don't, no breakfast?"

"I guess not," Dale joked. "She didn't give me any bargaining options."

"Well, before we get to her business proposal, did she say anything about us? That's the real reason you talked to her, isn't it? To find out what she knows?" Rodney asked, interrupting his meal. "I mean, did she see anything while we were building the shanty? Or worse, did she see anything dealing with Badgett?"

"No, she didn't. Well, there is one thing, and I'll come to that in a minute. Like I said, she was gone most of the summer, so she didn't have much chance to see us building our shanty. Plus, you can't see down to the river from her house. I checked on that while I was standing on her porch. You can't see anything past the lumberyard's rear gate. You can only see the river itself way downstream once it passes behind the last storage shed. Beyond that point she has a good view of the river but not before."

"Still, from what you've said, it sounds as though she was back home by the time we had to deal with Badgett. That's what really worries me. Did she see me kill Badgett or see the two of us move his body? Because he certainly yelled loud enough for her to hear across the street, and as you just said, she's able to see as far as the yard's rear gate. And that's exactly where I caught up to him."

"No, she didn't see us then, either. But she did see the police search the yard several days later, and Agnes Badgett was with them. Apparently, Agnes didn't treat the Federation police any better than she treats other people, at least not from what Delia could hear. She thought for sure the police would come over to her place to question her, but they didn't."

"Do you know why they didn't? That could be important."

"I do. And that brings me to the good part ... good for us, at least. Shortly after they left the lumberyard, they arrested the guard Badgett had hired to watch over it once he was forced to close the business. He was also supposed to keep an eye on Delia's house while she was in Pittsburgh. The guard's name is Ellis Grant. The police arrested him after Agnes insisted on it. She claimed that a day or so before Walter went missing, he had fired this Grant guy for not doing his job. And that, it seems, was enough for the police, the prosecutor, and the judge. The Federation police hauled Grant in, got him to confess, and then put him through one of their quickie trials. After that, off he went to a work camp. Case closed. I suppose his family, if he had one, is now in one of those big shelters for destitute families."

"Well, you're right. That is good for us but not for that poor son of a bitch. Innocent, as apparently only we know, but forced to confess anyway. So, according to these reports from Delia, the Feds convicted him of a murder without even being able to verify that a murder had actually been committed, since they've never recovered Badgett's body. Or did they?"

"No, it doesn't seem like they even searched the river. Most likely we would have seen them if they had. Or worse, they would have seen us. Delia says the detectives themselves never went beyond the rear gate while they were in the yard, at least not that she saw. And she heard a report later, on one of the pirate radio stations that have started popping up around the area, that Badgett's body was never found. So, no corpse. Seems like the police were more anxious to get Agnes to shut up than they were to find out what really happened."

"And by accusing the guard, she made it easy for them. Wonder what will happen to the lumberyard now?"

"Agnes will probably sell it, if I know her. She wouldn't be the type to try to operate it again, even if the Federation allowed her to reopen it. She'd just want the money it would bring her. That's my guess."

"If she does sell, it will probably be at a big profit, since lumber can't be harvested any more, even though demand for it is sky-high. All of Badgett's material has shot up in price just while sitting there. The Federation will surely authorize somebody to sell the materials for making repairs to older structures while charging whoever buys the yard a big fat licensing fee to operate it, even after Mrs. Badgett gets her cut."

"Well, as long as I have the gate key, they won't be charging us."

"Hopefully, we're done with building materials, but better not mention that key to your friend, Delia, no matter how much you trust her. One thing leads to another, you know. Besides, the new owner will most likely install new locks this time." Rodney was sitting on the edge of his bunk now, finishing the last morsels of the ham sandwich while paying close attention to Dale's every word.

"No, I didn't mention the key, and I won't. Didn't tell Delia where we're living, either, or in what, even though she is curious about it. But I do think we can trust her." Dale paused a moment, considering the gravity of Rodney's warning, then he continued, "I was careful not to say anything about the yard or the shanty. But just think of what's happened today, Rodney." Excitement now swelled in Dale's voice. "Two pieces of good news for us in one day— Badgett's disappearance solved to the satisfaction of both the police and his bitchy old wife and after that, Delia's business proposal. It's been a long time since either of us has had luck like this, hasn't it?"

"Certainly seems that way," Rodney replied.

"Well, what do you think of the plan Delia's come up with?" Dale continued. "Don't you think it could work?"

"Sounds promising, I have to admit. And it would be so easy to pull off … that is, if everyone could still use cash. But since they can't, Delia will be taking on some enormous risks by using her own bank account and phone. If she's caught, she'd be accused of running an illegal repair service. And truthfully, she'd be as guilty as sin in today's legal climate. No matter how much people need and want such a service, the Federation would consider it illegal. As for us, we'd be seen as her accomplices, and we'd be guilty, too. So, the Feds would pack both of us off to a labor camp without further discussion just as they would Delia. And her little boy. Sammy, is that his name?"

Dale nodded. "That's right, Sammy."

"Well, he'd end up belonging to the state, a ward of the state they call it, same as the poor kids on the shanty we saw after the guard shot their parents. And that would eventually mean child labor for Sammy, too, at least when he's old enough. Rough way to grow up, don't you think?"

"I see your point, but still, don't you think it's worth the risk just to be able to provide for ourselves again? That would be a big step above shantyboat life."

"True, but even if Delia's plan works—actually, especially if it works—we'd still need to visit the canteen and the shelter periodically just in case things do go wrong for some reason."

"Delia thought that might be the case. I told her you would know for sure."

"Well, she guessed right, because going on and off the Federation's various welfare plans would only serve to arouse suspicion about us, and suspicion leads to investigations, and, if nothing else, would likely result in a cancellation of benefits. Then we'd be on the streets with no way to get food and clothing except by stealing them and have only the shantyboat for our shelter, both day and night regardless of the weather. If that happened, we'd be better off in a labor camp with that poor guy, Ellis Grant. So, we'd be wise, once or twice a week, to use the canteen and shelter if only to keep our benefits activated. Besides, since we'd be working again and visiting people's homes, we'd need to shower and get fresh clothes more often. Can't do either of those living only on this shantyboat."

"But with money, we'll be able to buy our own clothes."

"You mean, Delia would be able to buy them for us. Remember, we don't have bank accounts."

"Okay, that's true, but it comes to the same thing, doesn't it? We would get what we need pretty much when we need it."

"I suppose it does, just a little more convoluted. But two things trouble me about Delia's plan, in addition to our becoming so dependent on her for everything. First is the start-up money. If Delia is nearly out of money, as she told you, how will she buy parts and fuel and the other things we'd need to get this business going?"

"I'm not sure. She says she does have some money that she brought back with her from her husband this summer, but it's running out. She's been trying to stretch it out just to survive, but that can only go on for so long until all the money is gone, unless new money can be brought in by this service business."

"Okay, but it takes time for any new business to get cash flow going, even with the speed of digital transactions today. And my second concern is her husband. What happens if he shows up all of a sudden?"

"I asked about that. She told me not to worry about him. She said that he's her concern and that she'll take care of him if he does return. And one more thing—she wants me to stay with her and Sammy for protection from squatters and robbers and such."

"You mean, move in with her? Is that what she wants?" Now it was Rodney's turn to be astonished. "She certainly moves fast. I'll say that for her."

"Yes, because she's especially afraid of squatters this winter. Seems she's already had someone try to break in a short while ago. She managed to scare him off, but she's afraid some desperate squatters might try again this winter and she won't be so lucky."

"Well, I'm not surprised she wants you to stay with her, and probably for more reasons than protection. But how can she be so sure her husband won't turn up? That part still puzzles me. Does she know something about him she's not telling you?"

"I don't think so."

"Well, just suppose there really is a good reason for his silence, that he really hasn't deserted her, at least not in his mind, and then that reason—whatever it is—goes away and suddenly he returns home. He puts his key in the lock and opens the door only to find another man—namely, you—holding onto his pretty wife. Here he comes home hoping to surprise her and be her hero, and instead *she*—and most of all *you*—surprise *him* instead. He wants to impress her with the money he's saved up, wants to play with his little boy again, and make love with his sexy wife again, and instead of all that, there you are, spoiling the whole thing, betraying him, the very man who was your supervisor. Then what happens? Probably not a romantic embrace with Delia or a friendly handshake with you. That'd be my guess."

"Well, if that happens, Delia will have to choose between Randy and me, that's all, assuming things don't get violent first."

"But why wouldn't they? Do you really think that's what she meant by saying she'd take care of him, that she'd do that with violence in some way? That she would strike first? Or just that she'd choose you and tell him to hit the road, and he would do it without a fuss? That she'd say, 'Oh, I don't need you any more, Randy. I have my own business now, and this fellow here in my arms, your former coworker, he is now my employee *and* my lover. Oh, and by the way, I have another employee nearby, and that means there's no room for you in this business, so scram.' Do you really suppose Randy would just walk away from his son and his home and his wife if she told him to? Just go away without a fight?"

"I honestly don't know what would happen, Rodney. No way for me to know for sure. But I do know that I'm willing to risk it, whatever might happen. Delia needs help right now, and she can't rely on Randy any more, hasn't even heard from him. Without our help ... well, she'll be out in the street this winter along with her little boy. But with her plan we can stop that from happening and help ourselves at the same time. Besides, another chance like this might never come along for either of us, not with the way things are today. Think about it, we could die right here in this shanty. Who knows, maybe even get shot just like those poor people we saw the day we met. That's what I think, and that's why I'm going to agree to her plan. So, are you with me?"

Rodney stood up slowly in the center of the cabin, stooping to avoid bumping his head on its low ceiling. He scratched the stubble on his chin while choosing his words thoughtfully. "These things you've mentioned, Dale—the things that Delia told you about this morning—about the unlicensed radio stations, the secret farmers' market, and this plan of hers for an undercover handyman service— all these things, plus our own shantyboat here—they are all of them little rebel encampments encroaching on the border of the Federation's totalitarianism. If the Federation detects any of these things and thinks for one tiny second that any one of them is a real threat to its power, as it probably would, or even just thinks they are an embarrassment to its image as the omnipotent state, as they surely are—then it will crush those offenses without mercy. I'm surprised the Federation police haven't tracked down those radio stations by now."

"Delia said something about the radio stations being mobile somehow and broadcasting mostly at night. I guess they use trucks to keep moving around."

"Well, the Feds will eventually track them down, if they really feel they need to. Since there aren't that many vehicles on the streets any more, they'll spot them eventually. And they will do that, because each of these things we're talking about is an example of the natural freedoms of mankind at work, freedoms given to us by God, if a person still dares to think about it that way, in divine terms, that is, let alone say it out loud. They are truly natural freedoms. Let's at least say that much and say it boldly. Say that these are freedoms, individual and economic, that we have a right to exercise in order to live lives fitting for human dignity. People need these freedoms to be really human and not be reduced to livestock kept in a pen by a Federation master who slops them twice a day at a canteen-trough on a fixed schedule and then beds them down at night in his community shelter-barn, and finally puts them to sleep with a propaganda fairy tale told on a giant screen TV. That's all we are right now—livestock, not people—and even that with no particular purpose.

"These natural freedoms can be suppressed, of course, just as they have been at times in the past and just as they are right now. Suppressed violently at times. But not extinguished. Despite everything, they're still alive in us. They've survived, just waiting for the right moment to spring up again, like the seeds of desert plants growing and flowering in a flash of sunlight after a thunderstorm. It's an amazing thing when you think about it, Dale, it really is. Miraculous, in fact, that people are still willing to risk their lives to be free, to have human dignity.

"So, I admire your friend, Delia. Hats off to her, I say, for her ingenuity and for her bravery! She's only asking us to do what used to be normal and natural, that is, to bring useful skills to the marketplace to satisfy needs people have. That's how it was before the Federation came into being. To make a living for yourself and your family, you had to have a skill or a profession in order to contribute value to the marketplace, through your job or through a business of your own. Now the Federation encourages people to look at the marketplace and say, 'Who will provide for me, who will take care of me?' And the Federation answers, 'Just obey and you'll be provided for.' Of course, the Feds do that by stealing from people who have created market value. And now, since those people have all but disappeared, the Feds just print money instead to keep the government running.

"But maybe a plan like Delia's can produce a rebirth of a real marketplace. Maybe that's what we're seeing with her plan and the other black market activities she mentioned. Maybe, maybe not. But in spite of my doubts—and I do still have them—in spite of all the reasons I've just mentioned for saying no, my answer, Dale, is yes. Yes, I'll help with Delia's plan."

"That's great, Rodney! I hoped you would, and thank you for doing it. Then let's go tell her. Let's tell her right now."

"No. No, you go alone. It's you she wants to stay with her and protect her and her little boy. And I don't blame you for wanting to be with her, too. Besides that, I would just be a fifth wheel, and I don't want that. We've put a lot of ourselves into this shantyboat, you and I—our sweat, the risk of being caught and sent off to a work camp, and, unfortunately, the blood of two other human beings mixed up in it, as well, even though we never wanted that to happen. After all we've done, I'm not ready to give up this shanty. Maybe if I did get an opportunity to live again with a woman in a warm house and a soft bed as you seem to have with Delia, I probably couldn't resist, either. There'd be no good reason to. But either way, I don't blame you for going, not at all. As for me, I'm staying here, at least for now. So, you go. Go to her right away. I'm sure she's waiting for you this very minute!"

Chapter 16: Together

When Dale arrived at Delia's home later that afternoon, it was beginning to get dark. As he crossed the street to her porch, he saw a blue panel truck with "Cal's Delivery Service" painted in white letters on its side. It was parked in the driveway at the rear of her house. The drive led to a detached garage, an outdated feature from long ago in new homes but one that was nevertheless still very common in this older part of town.

He mounted the steps to the porch and before he could knock, Delia threw open the door and greeted him. Now she was wearing a dark blue dress, very tight at the hips and bodice. Her skin and hair had a spicey winter fragrance. *Probably cinnamon*, Dale thought.

"Well, did you see it?" she asked while grabbing his right arm with both of her hands and pulling him inside. "Did you see the truck in the driveway?" She was bursting with excitement.

"I did, I sure did. So, you got it already?"

"Yes, and no problem, either. Cal thought my daily rental proposal was a great idea. His family can still use the van on weekends that way. When he seemed so agreeable, I took the chance that your answer would be yes and paid him for tomorrow. So, is your answer yes?"

"Absolutely, it is!"

"And what about your friend, Rodney? Is he in, too?"

"He agreed, also. Not only did he like your plan, but he also said you must be a very smart and brave lady to have come up with it."

"Great, I'm glad he thinks so, because I already have five jobs lined up for the two of you tomorrow—all so close by that you could actually walk to them if you didn't have heavy tools to carry."

"Wow, you don't waste any time, do you?"

"The sooner we get started, the sooner we have money coming in—or the bits and bytes that pass for money these days. Most of these jobs are really small repairs. So, you'll have to do lots of them before the money adds up to anything significant."

At that point Sammy came thumping down the stairs, wearing shoes this time. "Hello, Mr. Nutter," he offered.

"Hello there, Sammy. Nice to see you again."

"Are you gonna stay with us tonight, Mr. Nutter? Mom said you might."

Dale looked at Delia, who offered no help except to ask, "Well, are you?"

"If your mom wants me to, Sammy, I will."

"O-kay, I already know she does! Then we can play a game after supper. Checkers!" Sammy was jumping up and down with excitement now. "I'm really good at checkers, Mr. Nutter. My dad taught me how to play when he still lived here."

"Then that's what we'll do, Sammy," Dale promised him. "We'll play checkers. Maybe you can teach me to be as good at it as you are."

"I'll teach you all I can, but I'm gonna win, I bet."

"Now you're in for it, Dale," Delia managed to say as they all started to move toward the kitchen. "I can't even count the number of checker contests I've lost to him."

"Oh, back to business for a minute," Dale said, stopping her on the way to the kitchen. "As for the tools, Rodney and I have collected most of what we need already. No toolbox to put them in, though, just a canvas bag or two we've found, like the ones we used in the lumberyard, but those will do for a start."

Dale immediately regretted referring to the lumberyard, but Delia seemed not to catch his gaffe. Instead of reacting to it, she replied, "There are also some tools in the basement Randy left behind. Maybe you guys can use some of those, too, so look at those. But when you're ready for a toolbox or even two, we'll get them and any other tools you need. Tomorrow I'll call some more people I know to see if they need any work done. As I talk to people, I'm asking each of them to call at least three or four of their friends to see if they might need repair work done, also, since we can't advertise publicly. Maybe in another day or two, we'll have people calling us instead of my having to call them. But tonight let's have a dinner to celebrate. Is Rodney going to join us?"

"No, said he didn't want to be a fifth wheel, but he will be here for breakfast tomorrow."

"Good, then I'll meet him at breakfast. I want to. And maybe afterward he'll feel comfortable enough to eat dinner with us after we meet tomorrow, but right now let's all go into the kitchen.

There's chili and corn bread waiting for us, or there will be as soon as I heat up the cornbread."

"Yes, Mom, let's go eat," Sammy shouted as he ran ahead into the kitchen. "I'm hungry!"

"He's always hungry," Delia remarked to Dale, laughing. "So, you and Rodney better bring in lots of money!"

As Dale sat down at the kitchen table with Delia and Sammy for the second time that day, he couldn't help but be amazed again at his sudden good fortune, a turn of fate that had come to him through the simple words carried on the winter wind, "Dale, is that you?" After more than a year on the streets, he could hardly believe that now he was sitting in a house again rather than in a canteen, at a table not a bench, eating thick chili with real meat and beans in it, not watery cabbage soup dotted with mushy carrot slices. Nor could he believe that tonight he would not be going to the shelter next to the canteen to parade naked through the basic human actions of choosing clean clothing, showering, and relieving his bowels and bladder—all in full view of his fellow vagrants and the shelter employees. So amazed that all this had happened to him, let alone happened within the time period of a single day, he didn't feel like a vagrant any more. But what he did feel, as Delia placed before him the steaming bowl of chili and a plate stacked with hot golden triangles of corn bread, was that somehow he should be giving thanks for this bounty which had so suddenly and generously appeared to him, expressing thanks to some force beyond his own control, for surely, he had not earned this good fortune by any effort of his own. Or was all this Delia's initiative alone? Oh, well, no one he knew gave thanks any more for anything. The Federation wouldn't approve.

After they had eaten a while, Dale's stomach told him to stop, so unaccustomed was he to the large amount of food he'd been given twice in one day. Delia's chili thickened with corn bread filled him completely and quickly.

"Don't like my chili?" Delia asked in a disappointed tone, seeing a flash of pain on Dale's face.

"No, no. Love it. Love it too much, in fact. Just not used to eating so much at one time any more. I guess my stomach's shrunk some over time. I'll have to retrain it if you're the cook. It's been a while since I've had the chance to have what we used to call a full meal."

"Well, then, I guess you won't want the cinnamon-chocolate pudding I made, either?" Delia feigned a sorrowful tone this time. "Guess I'll just have to eat your serving as well as mine."

"Oh, no, you don't!" Dale replied quickly. Then he struck his stomach lightly with the flat of his fist as though he were making a *mea culpa*. "There!" he declared, shaking his stomach now with both hands, or rather only pretending to, for there was an insufficiency of stomach to be shaken, at least not enough to give any real credence to his joke. Nevertheless, he declared, "Now I've made room for the pudding."

Sammy laughed at Dale's antics and then did the same to his own stomach, which was even more insufficient for shaking than Dale's, saying, "So did I, Mom. I made room for pudding, too. Now it's your turn."

"I'm not the one having stomach problems, boys," Delia replied, "but I will get the pudding—one serving for each of us, then, with whipped cream and cinnamon sprinkled on top."

As soon as they had all consumed their bowls of pudding and Sammy had wiped away his whipped cream moustache, none of which took all that long, Delia began to busy herself with cleaning up the kitchen while Sammy raced off to his room, only to return seconds later with a folded checkerboard under his left arm and a green velvet sack full of red and black checkers in his right hand. Grasping Dale's hand and pulling him away from Delia, he declared, "Time for checkers now, Mr. Nutter," and so led Dale from the delight of watching Delia move about the kitchen in her tight dress.

"Goodbye. See you soon, Dale," Delia said without turning from the sink as they left her and started toward the living room. "I'll come along to rescue you by-and-by."

Unfolding the checkerboard on the coffee table in front of the sofa, Sammy gave Dale a whimsical look and asked, "Have you ever played checkers for real, Mr. Nutter?"

"Yes, Sammy, I have, but that was a long time ago. Probably when I was your age," Dale answered, trying to remember if he'd

115

ever played with his own children, one of whom was only a year or so older than Sammy. "But I'll try my best," he added.

By the time Delia joined them, two games had been completed, Sammy winning both in short order. "Well, then, little Mr. Checker Champ, it's about time for your bath, I'd say."

"Ah, can't I skunk him one more time, Mom? He's easy."

"I think life has skunked him enough recently, Sammy. Let Mr. Nutter rest a while. Besides, he has a busy day waiting for him tomorrow, he and his friend, Mr. Tanner. We need them to be at their best." After a mild protest, Sammy gathered the checkers back into the velvet bag, folded the checkerboard, and climbed the stairs, stamping a bit louder than necessary in mild protest.

"And don't skimp on your bath, young man," Delia called after him. "I know very well how long it should take." Then smiling at Dale, she took his left hand in both of hers, which were still damp from her kitchen work. She looked quickly at his left wrist on which he was wearing Walter Badgett's watch, though barely visible under the cuff of his sleeve, before fixing her eyes on his. Then she asked playfully, seductively, "Well, now for you, Mr. Handyman, have you decided where you'd like to sleep tonight—on this sofa or in my bedroom?" She cupped her right hand over the watch as if to disregard it.

Completely oblivious to Delia's inspection of his wrist, Dale answered in a whisper, "I think you already know."

"I hope I do, but I want you to say it." She whispered, "Say it for me."

"Then, I will. I want to be with you." And with that reply, he pulled her close and kissed her, on the mouth this time, and then kissed her, again and again, and began unbuttoning the bodice of her dress before the ringing of her telephone interrupted them. Delia rose quickly to retrieve the phone, which she'd left on the kitchen counter. Dale could hear her voice in exchange with the person on the other end. The call ended with Delia repeating an address and saying, "Okay, I believe I know where that is. They should be able to reach you no later than 2:00 PM tomorrow. Just be aware the repair may require a second visit. Is that okay with you? Great. They'll be there, but one of us will call you first to confirm, okay?"

Delia returned to the sofa, carrying her cell phone with her this time and saying as she placed it on the coffee table, "I'll have to learn to keep this thing close by from now on—now that we're in business. I'm not used to getting so many calls. That was the first customer to contact us directly. Now you have six appointments tomorrow, and you'll need the panel truck for sure."

Dale heard the happiness in her words yet at the same time didn't because he was transfixed by the sight of her blouse still unbuttoned and spread open, revealing to him the cleavage at which Walter Badgett had so often and so obviously ogled, and which he himself, he had to admit, had longed to touch even when his wife and children were still with him. But trying to refocus, he said, "Do you really think people will put up with second trips, since we won't have any parts yet?"

"Yes, I think so. I thought about that, and I've warned the people I've spoken with about that possibility, as I did just now. I told them we're just starting up and don't have an inventory of parts yet. Probably we never will. They all seem to understand. All they really want is just someone to help them, so keep a good list of the parts you'll need. We can afford to double up on a few of the smaller parts you'll need frequently, just to save on fuel and time. I'll give you a pen and notebook to take along.

"Also, tomorrow give me your clothing sizes, yours and Rodney's both. We'll get you two some proper work clothes of your own so that you don't have to rely on hand-me-downs and reworked rags from the local shelter. Oh, and as soon as Sammy is in bed, the bathroom is yours. I bathed before you came."

"I could tell," he said. "You smell so fresh and clean." They kissed again. She leaned her head back and let him kiss her breasts now until Sammy called out from upstairs, "Okay, Mom, I'm done."

———•○•———

That night Delia welcomed Dale to her bed with even more eagerness than she had displayed when she learned that he and Rodney had accepted her work proposal. With her bare arms and legs clasped around him in the darkness, she whispered to him, "Stop worrying about Randy. I know you still are. I could still see the concern in your eyes and feel the hesitation in you now. But if Randy wanted me, he'd be here holding me now instead of you. But he's not. It's time for both of us to put him out of our minds and live

117

a new life—together. You're mine now, Dale. Now make me yours."

At midnight Dale was still awake, reliving the pleasures he had received and given with the woman beside him. She was sleeping soundly while still clinging to his arm with both hands, just as she had done when he arrived. He dared not move for fear of awakening her. Still, the flood of thoughts created by this most extraordinary day kept his mind buzzing and sleep at bay. Could this sudden passage from unrelenting nightmare to domestic comforts and carnal pleasures be real? If he fell asleep now, would all of this be gone when he awakened, vanished into nothingness and the nightmare of his recent life return? No matter what, he wouldn't let that happen. *Tomorrow*, he resolved, *we'll make good on today's promises.*

Chapter 17: Work

Every time he descended the hill from Camden Avenue to the riverbank where the shantyboat was tied, Rodney was pleased by the shanty's concealment—far enough from the street to avoid anybody even being tempted to look in its direction, down the hill, out of sight, and behind a dense screen of trees, mostly willows and sycamores, that lined both sides of the river east of Parkeston. Even leafless as the trees were now, the thicket of their branches still largely concealed the shantyboat.

Ascending the hill from the shanty this morning and passing through the overgrown vacant lot he and Dale used to reach the street, he thought, *Freedom is worth this inconvenience, this subterfuge, and I'm not going to give it up.* He felt this way even though he was hampered today by the heavy canvas bag slung over his shoulder, which was filled with most of the tools he and Dale had accumulated to build the shantyboat. Here he was, on his way to work for the first time in nearly four years.

But he was also thinking to himself this morning as he set out for Delia's house, *I'll need to replace my watch now that I'm working again. Dale kept Badgett's watch. But now I'll need one, too, since time of day, the day of the week, even the date of the month will have meaning again.* He couldn't remember any longer what had happened to his own wristwatch, just that it was gone, probably lost one night in one of the shelters as he showered. *Should have hidden that watch with the knife each night,* he thought. *Maybe I could get a watch from a pawnshop. Bet those places are bursting with cheap items of all kinds these days.*

Rodney arrived at Delia's house promptly at seven, even without the aid of a wristwatch. Dale, watching from the living room window, saw him as he crossed the street and stood ready at the door to greet his friend. He called out to Delia as Rodney approached, "Here he comes. And he's toting our tools. Glad he remembered to bring them."

But Delia was upstairs busily instructing Sammy on how to greet "Mr. Tanner" and didn't reply until she came down the stairs with Sammy in tow and saw Rodney. After the exchange of introductions and Sammy's performing perfectly to his mother's instructions, Delia led everyone to the kitchen, where she served

119

them a breakfast of pancakes and bacon. Sammy was quick to soak his single but large pancake with faux maple syrup, while Dale and Rodney focused on the very real and thick bacon with great pleasure.

"Delia, where did you manage to find this bacon?" Rodney asked. "I haven't eaten any for the past two years, let alone bacon cut this thick. It must be rare as Beluga caviar these days."

"Ah, I have a secret source. Can't tell you where, but here's a clue. You've walked by it every day on your way to and from the men's Southside canteen and shelter area and just didn't realize it."

"So, you mean a black market butcher shop, then?"

"Is there any other kind with things as they are now? The meat cases in the Federation's grocery stores are empty most of the time, but not where I go. New marketeers of all stripes are springing up all over the place, even though they have to operate in secret locations, advertise on the q. t., and specialize in only a limited range of products. Nevertheless, I believe there will soon be so many of them that the Federation won't be able to contain them all. In fact, I wonder if they even want to contain them now. I'm nearly of the opinion that by turning their attention from these black marketeers, the Feds believe they are able to avoid mass protests over the lack of staples, which is the result of their own failures from trying to impose centralized planning on the economy. They see the black market operations as a sort of relief valve."

Then Dale offered, "I guess since Rodney and I haven't exactly been in a position to buy anything for such a long time, we haven't heard about these places."

"Well, I can assure you that they do exist," Delia said. "More and more of them each month, it seems. But so far all of them are small and specialized. Some of them even have to move from location to location to protect themselves. One sells vegetables, another sells meats, and still another staples like flour and sugar. All advertised, if you can call it that, only by word-of-mouth. Makes you understand how general stores and later on supermarkets got started—to help their customers avoid the inconvenience of going to so many different places."

"And hopefully, those supermarkets will come back to full strength someday," Rodney added. "Especially if the Federation is willfully ignoring these black market operations, as you say, Delia. Soon, one of those marketeers will find a way to sell meat and vegetables and staples—all in one place—so that he gets a greater share of the marketplace versus his other, smaller black market competitors, to say nothing of the state-sponsored stores. But a crackdown by the Federation will come at some point, I'm afraid, once the Feds believe that the risk of allowing the black marketeers to expand offers a greater danger to Federation controls than the risk of food riots if the black market operations are closed down."

"What's a black market?" Sammy asked while spearing the last bit of his soggy pancake with an adult-size fork he held at mid-handle.

"A place where things people need are sold without being controlled by the government," Delia answered him. "But don't ever say those words 'black market' to anyone outside this house, Sammy. The government people don't like that. Understand me? That could get us all into trouble."

Already scared into silence by his mother's warning, Sammy shook his head in somber agreement.

"Well," Dale said, glancing at Walter Badgett's watch, "We should get started on our appointments."

"Yes, I'm anxious to get going," Rodney added. "And thanks for the breakfast, Delia. It was wonderful to have a meal away from the canteen, especially with meat included."

"Oh, you're both welcome. But before you go, I have some important instructions for you. On the lampstand beside the front door, you'll find the keys to the panel truck, a cell phone, and the list of today's appointments with their addresses and phone numbers. There's also a notepad and pen beside them. Use those to make notes about parts you might need and anything else that comes up. My phone number is written on the pad cover. If the need is urgent, call me and I'll see if I can get the parts right away. When you finish one job, call the next to tell them you're on the way. The more we talk with our clients, the more they'll accept us and rely on us and help us advertise our service. You build trust and grow a customer base by reliably carrying out the easy tasks first—like calling ahead and then showing up on time, always doing what you say you'll do."

"Yes, Boss Lady, we got it," Dale said with a laugh. "You know, you're a lot tougher than Walter Badgett ever was."

121

"Good, glad to hear it." Delia said. "And another thing, have the customers send their payment information to your phone first. That way, you can review it to make sure it's correct. Then forward it to my phone, and I'll deposit it into our account."

"That fast?" Rodney asked.

"Exactly, that fast," Delia said with an affirming nod. "The sooner we have the money, the better. Also, it's necessary for avoiding a large deposit at the end of the day that might attract Federation scrutiny, especially if we had a pattern of such deposits—that is, large amounts transacted about the same time of day and done repeatedly."

"Yes, Dale mentioned that to me," Rodney interjected. "Very clever of you, Delia. Keeping our services under the surveillance radar. Very well thought out."

"Thanks," Delia replied. "But one last thing, guys. If any customer is agreeable to purchasing parts or materials in order to speed up the repairs, have them do it. I've also listed the phone numbers of the closest plumbing and electrical suppliers on the notepad, the only ones that are still in business, so the list is short. Just help the customers to order the correct item from the correct supplier. The suppliers will hold orders for twenty-four hours, so you can probably pick up the items in the afternoon and then return to the customer's home for the repairs either later today or first thing tomorrow. Just be careful what you say to the supplier representatives, however. These are all Federation sponsored businesses, after all. They are the only ones still doing business.

"Also, when you get back here at the end of the day, we'll work on tomorrow's schedule. Then I'll call the customers to let them know when to expect you. I'll probably even have some new appointments by that time. Oh, and I've got some leftover ham sandwiches for you two in the fridge, and I made a thermos of coffee and two cups for you to take along with you today. Got all that?"

Grinning, Dale said, "I do, but you sure are a tough boss, Delia."

Not grinning, Delia replied, "I know, but we have to make sure this venture of ours succeeds, and since we have to rely on customer referrals to build our business rather than using public advertising, we have to do everything we can to make them happy and trust us and help us spread the word about our service."

"That's all great advice, Delia," Rodney said. "That's how businesses should always operate. And we'll follow your instructions to the letter. Well, Dale, shall we get going?"

———————————

As they walked to the panel truck, Dale carrying the thermos and ham sandwiches and Rodney toting the bag of tools he'd left on the porch, they joked about whether either of them could even remember how to drive. It had been that long.

"Well, I have the keys, so I'll try first," Dale offered while unlocking the truck.

"And while you're trying to recall how to drive," Rodney joked as he placed the tools in the back of the truck, "guess I'll just close my eyes and pray a little." Then he added in a serious tone, "Wait a minute. Do you even have a valid driver's license any more? I believe mine's expired, now that I think of it, so I'd become a liability to us if I drove and we were stopped by the Feds. And renewing a license could mean an end to vagrant benefits—no more canteen, no more shelter—because a driver's license renewal means you're working for yourself or someone else, and working means no benefits."

Dale stopped, pulled from his pocket a badly frayed wallet, and checked. "Oh, no, mine expires in about three weeks," he reported. "Good thing you thought of licenses, Rodney. I hadn't bothered with it, since there was no opportunity for me to drive and few vehicles left to drive anyway. Guess I'll be staying with Delia for sure, because at least one of us needs to renew."

"Then you're definitely driving," Rodney said, laughing. "Guess I'll have my eyes shut all day and get reacquainted with God."

Dale backed the panel truck onto Pinecrest Street, which ran beside Delia's house and intersected Camden Avenue opposite the gate to the lumberyard. It led up a gentle grade to several clusters of houses, most of them similar to Delia's. The street did, in fact, have a crest. Pine trees, however, if there ever were any, were nowhere to be found.

On their way to the first appointment, a short drive to a house with a running toilet, Rodney said, "Delia's quite well-organized, just as you said. It's as though she's done this kind of thing before."

"Probably due to her bookkeeping and bank auditing experience," Dale offered. "She must have written up all these notes and numbers and put them on the stand, the one by the door, while I was showering last night, because I don't remember seeing her do any of that. She was probably in that room to the right of the stairwell. I think that's her office. Besides, afterward I kept her pretty busy."

"Did you, now? Well, what a surprise! But I don't think bookkeeping alone explains her skills. There's something more about her, I'd say, something controlling that worries me a little. But we'll see in due time, I guess. Wait, turn in here, Dale! We're at our first customer's already. Right there, that driveway on your left."

<hr/>

The morning round of appointments went smoothly. A toilet flapper and a kitchen faucet cartridge had to be ordered. That necessitated return visits that afternoon but resulted in quick installations. By the end of the day, the appointments had netted a total of $300 transferred to Delia and thence on to her bank account.

When they arrived back at Delia's, she greeted them from the back door of the kitchen as they walked from the truck. Sammy was standing next to her. "Great work, guys! You're conquering heroes! A terrific first day. Come on in this way, through the kitchen."

"It felt good as we were doing it, it really did," Dale said.

Rodney nodded his agreement, adding, "Yes, it felt especially good to be doing something useful again. Something people can appreciate and benefit from."

"Well, I can say for certain that it really was a good day," Delia said. "I followed up with each customer after you completed the work just to be sure they were satisfied and to remind them to refer us to other customers. All of them were thrilled that someone is doing this kind of work again, I can tell you that. And they all promised to help with referrals."

"What about the two who required the inconvenience of a second visit?" Rodney asked.

"Yes, even those. Actually, especially those. They were impressed by the same-day turnaround. And here's some more good news—tomorrow you have ten new appointments plus another six so far for later in the week. So, as you can see, guys, your appointment calendar is filling up fast. At this rate, you'll become rich and famous before you know it," she said, laughing.

"Actually," Rodney was quick to reply, "I hope no one else knows it if we do become rich, because it's much safer not to be famous these days, especially if you're also going to be rich."

"Well, the anonymous part can be managed by observing the surveillance thresholds and by opening multiple bank accounts as we need to. And that's just what you'll eventually have to do—that is, after payment in-kind gets you back on your feet." Once again, Delia had thought far ahead.

"And, Rodney," she added, "why don't you stay for dinner tonight? Let's all celebrate a little. I still have plenty of chili and corn bread left over from yesterday. The corn bread will just go stale if we don't eat all of it today."

"Sounds tempting. Dale told me what a great cook you are."

"Yes, I did," Dale confirmed, hoping his compliment would lead to a profusion of kisses later in the evening.

"Then that settles it. You two wash up while Sammy and I get the meal ready. Won't we, Sammy?"

"Yes, we will and pretty fast, too, 'cause I'm hungry!"

Chapter 18: Stray Cats

While Rodney accepted a second meal that day, he declined the opportunity to shower at Delia's. Instead, he trudged off into the dusk toward the community shelter and a change of clothes, hoping as always that he could find the sizes he needed.

The next morning, on his way back to Delia's, he was passing a vacant lot on the opposite side of the street from the one he normally used when a raucous noise drew his attention. In the lot, not far from the street, a clutter of abandoned and somewhat emaciated cats was busy sizing up one another and emitting hisses like steam from so many broken valves. Between them lay the prize carcass of what appeared to be a rat. All the cats, save one, were adults. But that one, a juvenile orange tabby, not much beyond kittenhood, was clearly intimidated by what its adult clutter mates were about to do. Meowing frantically at the sight of Rodney, it ran toward him through the grass and leaped over the trash strewn in the lot. The tabby seemed to be calling out to him for help. And so, he stopped to allow the cat to catch up to him, whereupon it sat at his feet and fell silent, staring up at him.

What should I do? Rodney thought. *The poor thing must be recently turned out, because it still thinks a human being can help it. It's not starving yet and even looks to be in pretty good condition. But it has no chance to compete with the adult cats for a taste of rat flesh. And that's probably a good thing. That rat carcass is very likely infested with poison, which explains why it's just lying there in a vacant lot in the first place.*

He reached down and picked up the cat, which made no attempt to avoid him, as though it expected its plaintive meowing to produce this very result, further proof that it had been recently abandoned, Rodney thought. It quickly nestled itself into the crook of Rodney's left arm, clinging with the claws of its forepaws onto his winter coat.

"Think you're pretty clever, don't you?" he said to the cat, which looked up at him again and responded with a different, softer meow that quickly gave way to a purr and a slow blink of its eyes. "But how can I help you? I mean, would you really be content living on a shantyboat? Do you really want to replace Dale? If you do, you could have an entire bunk to yourself. Wonder what Dale would think of that?" Rodney chuckled at that thought and resumed his walk with the cat still in his arms. "There is a bit of lumber left over. I suppose I could build a litter box with it. Was going to burn it in the stove but don't have to. And there's plenty of sand along the river for litter. I suppose we could scrounge up a bowl or two for food and water. Your companionship would be nice. But no, I shouldn't. It's not fair to either of us to pretend this way."

He stopped again, put the cat back on the ground, and started to walk away. The cat immediately resumed its sorrowful meowing and ran after him. He stopped again, picked up the cat again, and held it above his head this time to examine it.

"Okay, little guy, I should have guessed your sex, since you're an orange tabby. Well, you win. We'll give you a chance today but a one-day trial only. You'll go to work with Dale and me. But you'll have to behave yourself or back on the street you go, just another vagrant like the rest of us." He stroked the cat a few times and resumed walking, quicker now, trying to make up for lost time. The cat resumed purring, despite being jostled, and looked ahead expectantly over Rodney's left arm.

"Just hold on. We'll be there soon. Wonder what the boss lady will think of you?"

<hr />

When they arrived at Delia's house, Rodney along with the cat, Dale let them in.

"I brought along a new friend I met this morning," Rodney said. "Hope Delia doesn't mind. I think he wants to be your replacement, Dale. Wants to take over your bunk, at least on a tryout basis. I believe that's what he means by all this purring."

After tilting his head this way and that to examine the visitor, Dale concluded, "Well, he's better-looking than I am, I have to admit that. A bit smelly, though."

"Who is?" Delia asked, coming up behind Dale and putting her arms around his waist. "Good morning, Rodney. Who's a bit smelly? Oh, I see!" she exclaimed, seeing the cat. "He is better-looking than you in some respects, Dale," she said. "But not all." With that, she squeezed Dale's bicep affectionately and kissed him on the cheek.

"I thought we would at least give this little fellow a chance today and take him with us on our rounds," Rodney explained.

"Oh, no, you don't," Delia quickly interjected. "Here, let me have him for a minute." She took the cat from Rodney's hands. "Whew! You do smell, little boy! You've been in garbage somewhere and need a bath in the worst way." Then she whirled around and called out, "Sammy, come down here quick and see the cat."

Sammy came thumping down the stairs from his room as fast as he could go. "A cat? What cat?" he cried out.

"This cat, Mr. Tanner's cat," Delia said and put the cat's face close to Sammy's. "It's a tom cat, a boy like you, Sammy." Then, turning to Rodney, she asked, "Where did you find him?"

"Actually, he found me. Came running to me from a vacant lot just up Camden Avenue a bit. He wasn't doing all that well trying to join a pack of other cats that was about to battle over a dead rat."

Sammy's eyes widened as he asked, "Can we keep him? Can we, Mom?"

"No, Sammy, I said he's Mr. Tanner's cat." Then, still holding the animal, Delia turned back to Rodney. "Tell you what, though, Rodney. I'll make you a deal. Let us keep the cat here while you and Dale are out attending to the appointments. Sammy and I will scrub him up for you, feed him, and have him ready to go home with you this evening—all fresh and clean and smelling great. I don't think he'd help you all that much with electrical and plumbing repairs anyway."

"True enough," said Rodney. "And he'd probably enjoy your company more than ours. Just waiting for us in the back of the panel truck wouldn't be nearly as much fun as having a little boy to play with."

"Good. Then why not bring him back here every day you're working? You don't have a better place to keep him, do you? Oh, sorry, Dale told me not to ask about that. Said it could get me into trouble."

"No, I have an adequate place maybe but not a better one. Certainly not as good as your home."

"And it would be good for Sammy, who is going to learn to take care of this cat, aren't you, Sammy?"

"Really? You'd let me?"

"Sure. You're old enough now. It would be a good learning experience for you," she said to him. "Well, do we have a cat-sharing deal?" she asked Rodney, putting the cat down on the carpet so that Sammy could pet it.

"All right, but on one condition."

"Oh, and what would that be?"

"That Sammy comes up with a good name for the cat by this evening. Think you can do that for me, Sammy?" Rodney knelt beside the boy, who was busy petting the cat.

"I promise I will," Sammy replied, looking up at Rodney earnestly. "But can Mom help me if I can't think of a good name by myself?"

"Hmm. Okay, I suppose so, but only if she's willing to do it."

"We'll come up with an appropriate name, don't you worry," Delia was quick to say before adding, "And it won't be a simple Felix or Kitty-Kat, either."

With the immediate fate of the nameless cat settled for the day, Delia served the feline a saucer of milk and the rest of her charges a breakfast of bacon and eggs, once again to Rodney's amazement, troubled as he still was over Delia's relative abundance of financial resources versus her desperate claims of the poverty stalking her and her son. After breakfast, the two men set off on their new and greatly expanded round of appointments while Delia and Sammy tended to the cat and thought about exotic names.

———⊰·⊱———

That evening the men returned to Delia's after completing over three hundred and fifty dollars' worth of repair work. Delia had tracked their progress throughout the day as Rodney forwarded to her phone their customers' payment information so that she knew about where they were, where they were headed, and exactly how much they had earned. And when she wasn't tracking their progress and making bank deposits, she was preparing a set of surprises for them. So, when they entered through the kitchen door that evening, which they were using routinely now, she ushered them straight into the living room where their surprises waited.

"There," she said, pointing proudly to sets of merchandise as though they were presents under a Christmas tree, a largely neglected custom now. "All delivered about an hour before you got here." Before Dale and Rodney were two stacks of work clothes and underwear folded neatly and placed on the coffee table. And leaning against the table were two litter pans, two bags of cat litter, and two bags of dry cat food.

"Rodney," she said, "just to keep things simple, I got all your work clothes in olive with grey underwear, and, Dale, yours are the khaki work clothes with white underwear. Makes things easier at laundry time. That okay?" Both promptly agreed. "And the rest," she continued, "is for Jingle."

"Jingle?" Dale asked. Rodney just laughed.

"Yes, you know, Jingle the cat." Then Delia called upstairs to Sammy and told him to bring down Jingle. The two of them came trooping down the stairs, Sammy first with Jingle following until the cat saw Rodney. Then Jingle raced ahead of Sammy to sit at Rodney's feet. The cat now sported a fluffy coat and a fluorescent green collar to which was affixed a tiny but noisy bell.

Rodney picked up Jingle and flicked the bell twice before saying, "I see you've had a big day, Jingle. Gotten yourself all cleaned up and belled to keep you out of trouble and gotten an appropriate name to boot." Jingle seemed to answer Rodney with an agreeable meow before nestling into his favorite position along Rodney's left forearm, then turning his head to look at his other companions who were laughing at his responses.

"So, you've belled the cat, have you, Delia?" Rodney asked.

"Yes, we have. That's what Sammy and I accomplished today—a bell to keep Jingle from catching birds and a name to go with the bell."

"And a collar you can see a mile away," Dale noted.

"And see at night," Delia added. "It's fluorescent."

"I think you've done a great job, Sammy," Rodney said to the boy. "Thank you, and thanks to your pretty mom, too."

<hr />

After several weeks, Dale and Rodney began each workday with a full appointment calendar of ten repair jobs plus several follow-ups from the previous day that still needed replacement parts—a wall receptacle, a toilet seal, window caulking, some insulation strips for an exterior door to block the cold winter air, a new dead bolt lock to foil desperate squatters and would-be robbers. Their most complicated job was repairing a leaking water line in a basement that required purchasing a pipe cutter and some repair collars. As cash flow improved, they began purchasing a few extra repair items that experience was telling them they should have on hand to avoid return trips to their customers.

After some detailed discussions with Dale and Rodney about their repair capabilities, Delia was careful to screen out projects they couldn't handle and refer the disappointed callers instead to the local authorized Federation repair services, all of which had lengthy wait times, sometimes more than a month long. Each time she had to do this, she apologized profusely and cautioned the callers not to mention anything about this new and necessarily secret repair service to the Federation-sponsored companies. All complied willingly, happy to know that the next repair they required might be carried out quickly rather than after months of inconvenience and perhaps damage to their homes if left to wait on a state-sponsored service.

Another routine also was taking shape—that between Dale and Delia. Each night now he showered while she put Sammy to bed. Then she bathed and came to him. She would leave her fuzzy ice-blue winter robe draped over a chair near the bed, readily at hand if she required it to respond to Sammy's needs. Then, languorous and nude, she would slip beneath the covers, move next to Dale to share the warmth he had already imparted to the bed, and arouse him.

Delia! Wonderful Delia! he would think afterward. *So eager to command during the day and yet so willing to please at night.*

But he still wondered and worried. Mostly he worried about Randy but was careful now not to mention this concern to Delia. He knew from working with Randy that he had been proud of his wife's good looks, always eager to brag about them and inordinately jealous of anyone he felt might try to usurp his place with her. If you agreed with his assessment of Delia's sexiness, he became jealous. Yet if someone dared to disagree with him in any way—to say, for example, "Well, Delia is chunkier in the legs than my girlfriend" or "I think my wife has prettier eyes and hair"—Randy would fly into a rage and threaten the offender with physical harm. But most of all, Randy was tormented by Walter Badgett's obvious lust for Delia,

131

about which Randy knew he must do nothing. And the more heavily the Greater Depression weighed on the country, the bolder Walter Badgett was with Delia and the more enraged Randy became.

Now here was a new rival, a real one, a successful one—himself, Dale Nutter, recent vagrant, penniless and devoid of prospects, yet lying next to Randy Hodge's wife and every night loving her while she responded to him with her own amorous words and warm willing flesh but voiced not a word of concern about her missing husband.

Dale also wondered about their future together. What would they become? Something more than lovers? They had not discussed birth control, for example. She knew, of course, he offered none. But then what about her? She'd spent the entire summer with Randy. Surely, even in a cramped apartment with Sammy nearby, they had managed to have sex, probably many times. If Randy's performances in the privacy of the marriage bed came remotely close to matching his boasting in the workplace, there must have been plenty of opportunities for Delia to become pregnant. But obviously during the summer she hadn't. And now it was December. Did she have access to birth control and not tell Dale? But he hadn't asked, as though asking might break this wonderful spell. Birth control pills were very expensive now, so they were not something a woman would purchase unless she had a definite need for them.

So, could he, Dale, have already impregnated her? Did she have his child inside her right now, soon to swell to noticeable size? If so, is that what she wanted because she truly loved him? Or was it the five hundred dollars she wanted because she needed the money? Five hundred dollars the Federation government was willing to pay as an incentive to women to bear children again, payable upon proof of a successful birth and with no questions asked about the child's father. And with the full cost of the prenatal care and delivery paid by the Federation medical insurance—all to help offset the drastic decline in population across the country after the onset of the Greater Depression. And hadn't Delia said she was willing to do anything to avoid losing her home?

Perhaps it's better not to mention pregnancy right now, Dale reasoned. *Better just to keep her happy, content, and safe. That's all she seems to want. Let things sort themselves out, however they can, whenever they will.*

132

He moved but just enough to look at her beside him. Though asleep, or seeming to be, she responded by rolling toward him and grasping his arm at the bicep. This had become her favorite gesture of ownership with him. "You're not allowed to leave me" that grasp seemed to say, "never." And then, with scarcely another thought, he, too, fell asleep.

Earlier that evening Dale had driven Rodney in the panel truck up to the vacant lot where a path led to the shantyboat. Normally, they wouldn't take a chance like this, but tonight Rodney had to tote all of Jingle's paraphernalia jammed now into a large tote bag—the bag of litter, a bag of dry cat food, the litter box, a feeding bowl, a drinking bowl, and a bottle of water—to say nothing of Jingle himself. All of this, save the cat, provided by Delia's generosity.

Once they arrived at the vacant lot, it was nearly dark.

"Won't you need some help getting all that stuff down to the shanty?" Dale asked. "Want me to go with you?"

"No, better not. That would leave the truck just sitting here for everyone to see. No telling what might happen to it or who might see it and want to contact the Feds. You better just go. Jingle and I will find our way. Then, tomorrow morning, it'll just be the two of us hiking to Delia's, so no problem then. We'll just leave the tools in the back of the truck."

"Well, okay, you're probably right. You always are. Good night then, and good luck with Jingle. Hope he likes my bunk."

Chapter 19: River Interlude

Several weeks later, the winter sun found Rodney asleep on his bunk with Jingle curled across the top of his head. The sun tried its feeble best to warm the cabin, where the last bit of firewood in Walter Badgett's stove had turned to cold charcoal.

In the small comfort of the shantyboat, meager though it was, and the safety of its isolation, tenuous though that was, Rodney's mind had gradually begun to relax during these weeks of winter, gradually regaining perspective, realizing now just what enormous strain both he and Dale had been under while homeless. It was then that Rodney began to experience extraordinary dreams. Indeed, so profound did his sleep become that he descended each night through the circuitous valleys of the deepest sleep he had ever known. Deeper and deeper he plunged into another world, it seemed. At first it was a land of blissful rest filled with pleasant recollections of his previous life, a life spent in the Happy Times. He saw his shipmates from the Navy again, his wife and his children. They were all young and eager for life's unfolding, and they looked to him to lead them. Even otherwise forgotten childhood friends came to visit him as he dreamt. These blissful dreams came to him no doubt because of the enormous relief of his newfound freedom and the privacy and peacefulness to which both the shanty and Jingle were contributing each day.

But after several weeks more, his dreams began to darken, becoming visions of final things, an Ultimate Purpose and Judgment before which he was ushered, as a sacrificial animal to an altar, by the revengeful spirit of Walter Badgett. And those dreams terrified him. He'd bolt upright from his narrow bunk in the middle of the night, quivering with fear, eyes wide open, though dreaming still, looking about him, trying to find some familiar reference point that would allow him to regain his mental balance and climb out of this new hell. But he couldn't see the walls of the shantyboat's tiny cabin, couldn't even see Jingle asleep on Dale's bunk beside him. Instead, he only saw his visions still, just as if his eyes weren't open at all, visions more vivid than any before. Visions of people strewn along the riverbanks, their bodies askew, a tangle of arms and legs and torsos—men, women, and children of all ages. Their streams of blood mingling, flowing together like a red tributary into the little river where his shantyboat floated silently in the night.

And he heard a background noise, as well. An eerie hum emanating from everything about him, including from within himself. The sound of death he thought it was, including his own. That must be what the approach of death sounds like, he thought—this hum, this signal of mortality transmitted from everything, large and small, coming from everywhere about him, even within him, but especially from the corpses scattered along the riverbank. A hum, the wave of death itself, containing a message that no one else seemed to hear let alone understand. But in the mystery of his dream, he *could* understand it. It said to him: *That world you once knew, that sweet America—you did not deserve it! That abundance you once had—none of you who enjoyed it actually earned it. You received it from those before you and weren't even grateful for it when you got it but grabbed it and consumed it like a birthright about to expire. Reckless and thoughtless, you failed to protect your rights with your honor and your lives. You squandered them instead, conceding them one at a time in exchange for a life of ease, ease from hard work and initiative, ease from thinking, too, while others took everything away from you, bit by bit, so you wouldn't notice, and took it all to augment their own power. Now all that you had is gone, lost to you, New Adam, and lost to your families, and you are lost to them, banished forever into servitude and desolation and ignominious death. Now everyone is truly equal, as Parity demands, the only real Equality, the Supreme and Undeniable Equality—an equality in misery, hopelessness, and despair. Zero equals zero at last—the ultimate and indisputable parity.*

Then nausea and horror would rise inside him and sweep over him like an angry sea, flooding his heart with grief and fear, as though he were about to drown, overwhelmed by the storm's crushing waves. But that very same power would finally awaken him instead and allow him to see the shanty once more and hear the tinkle of a cat's tiny collar bell.

Yet in those moments of panic, sitting upright on his narrow bunk, he tasted death like a bitter arsenic disc laid on his tongue—the Charon's coin placed in the corpse's mouth. He could feel a sharp piercing pain in his abdomen and smell a purging fire spreading about him. Only gradually would reality return to him.

135

Only gradually would he become aware again of the shanty's gentle rocking on the waters of the little river and his own solitude by its bank. Then and only then, calmed by the river's motion before a new day could shine warmth down on the shanty and into its cabin, could he regain himself and sleep once more a dreamless, empty sleep this time in the few moments of peace left to him, not even hearing the tinkling of the tiny bell as a cat leaped across the narrow aisle of the cabin to stretch out against him for the last minutes of the night's warm rest—the decisive moments between death and awakening.

Chapter 20: Confessions

Late spring now and Delia was pregnant and had been for three months. Dale and Rodney were standing beside her in the kitchen at the end of another successful workday—a long string of them, months now, in fact. Even so, today Delia looked worried.

Dale asked her, "Did something happen, honey? You look like you've seen a ghost, maybe a host of them."

Ignoring him for the moment, she said to Rodney, "I think you should stay with us tonight."

"Why is that?" he asked, puzzled as much by her ominous tone as by the suggestion itself. "Why tonight?"

"First, tell me this," she replied. "Would you allow Sammy to keep Jingle tonight, since you won't stay with us? He's been asking if Jingle could stay and sleep on his bed some night. Would it be all right?"

"I guess so, if Jingle is okay with it." Jingle had heard Rodney's voice, left Sammy upstairs, and came into the kitchen to investigate. Rodney picked up his cat and held him so that they looked into each other's faces. Jingle mewed and touched Rodney's nose with his paw, nails retracted. Rodney squinted his eyes and said, "I think that means he's willing," but said it somewhat reluctantly. "And does this in turn mean I need to find another cat to keep me company and concede Jingle to Sammy?"

"Oh, no, no. We wouldn't do that to you. It's just something Sammy has been pestering me about—having Jingle stay over. I meant to ask you earlier. I suspect one night with a cat on his bed will be enough for Sammy. It's entirely another reason why I think you should stay with us tonight—a much more important reason than Sammy wanting time with Jingle."

"Oh, and what's that?"

"You haven't heard what happened earlier today, downtown by the old park outside the floodwall?"

Both Rodney and Dale stiffened with concern, both recalling at once what they had witnessed there the day they first met. "No, we haven't heard a thing. What happened?" Dale asked.

Delia sat down at the kitchen table and began her explanation. "This morning I was scanning the radio dial to find one of those pirate stations I've been telling you about when I heard a frantic voice over the airwaves. I tuned in to it just as the announcer, one I've heard before, was saying that he'd learned from secret sources—that's what he called them—that the local Federation authorities had decided to clean out the colonies of shantyboats that have developed along the river. I think the radio announcer said there were ten shanties now just by the floodwall alone, as well as others upriver, mostly by the East Street Bridge. He even claimed to be able to see the ones tied up downtown from where he was at that time by using binoculars."

"But what happened?" Dale asked again with some impatience this time.

"The authorities brought in a Coast Guard speedboat equipped with a machine gun. While the broadcaster was watching, it came down the Ohio and pulled alongside the shanties. Without any warning, it started shooting. It shot up all ten of the boats in a matter of minutes, going methodically from one to another, he said. The radio announcer witnessed the whole thing and broadcast it as it was happening. His sources had told him this might happen—both where and when—so he had gotten into position to report it. He said all the boats either caught fire from being strafed or were set on fire by the Coast Guardsmen with torches they threw onboard. Some of the boats broke up and sank right away. Others broke loose from their moorings and drifted out into the Ohio River while they were still burning. Using his binoculars part of the time, the announcer said he saw dozens of people killed outright, right then and there—entire families including their children and pets. He also saw some of them falling into the river when the machine gun bullets tore through the boat cabins, hitting the ovens and stoves inside and starting fires. Some people managed to scramble ashore but were shot anyway. People were obviously screaming, the announcer said, though he was too far away to hear them. Soon, scores of dead bodies were floating beside the burning shanties—all drifting into the Ohio.

"I listened to the whole thing. It reminded me of that famous radio broadcast of the Hindenburg disaster. That was over a hundred years ago. The announcer kept describing what was happening as long as he could, even though his voice was breaking at times with emotion. He kept going like that until he had to move, because he was afraid of getting caught if he stayed where he was much longer. The whole thing was horrible, like nothing I've ever heard. Glad I didn't have to see it, even though in a way I did see it, because the announcer's description was so vivid. So, Rodney, that's why I think tonight would be a good night for both you and Jingle to stay here. The Coast Guard will probably come back searching for more shanties upriver."

Dale and Rodney looked at each other in shock before Rodney spoke up, still holding onto Jingle and stroking him. "I was afraid something like this would happen eventually to the shanty people. The shanties have become freedom boats, you know, freedom for people who have nothing else. All those people want in life is to be free of the Federation shelters and canteens, at least some of the time. That and to have some privacy for themselves and their families each night. And now they've died for wanting even that little bit of freedom. All because totalitarians can't tolerate freedom, not even the smallest sign of it, let alone having a river starting to fill up with colonies of freedom boats."

Then Dale asked, "So, somebody tipped off the radio station, and that allowed them to find a place where they could watch this happen and even know the timing for it?"

"Yes, that's what the radio announcer claimed, but the people in the shantyboats didn't know," Delia responded. "Why do you suppose nobody warned them? Lives could have been saved."

"Good question," Rodney said, "but don't know the answer. Might not have been possible to tell them in time. Or maybe because the source of the information had to be protected. Either way, the incident shows that cracks are developing in the Federation's fortress walls, and they are willing to use extreme measures to stop those cracks from widening. Dale, have you ever told Delia what happened the day we met?"

"No, I didn't want to trouble her with that."

"But now would be a good time to tell her, don't you think?"

"Yes, I suppose it would."

"What?" Delia asked, looking from one to the other with an anxious face. "What are you two talking about?"

Dale began the story of meeting Rodney in the park by the floodwall and their witnessing the murders of two people on a shantyboat and the abandonment of their two orphaned children by a Federation guard. "And we didn't dare tell anyone about it, Delia, for the same reason I've never told you where Rodney and I were living," Dale said, concluding his story. "Knowing the truth and repeating it can get you into big trouble sometimes."

"That's right," Rodney added. "Even though reporting what the guard had done would normally be the right thing to do, it would have been the end of us if we had. So, I expect the radio announcer and his crew were in a similar dilemma. They probably have Federation police chasing after them every day as it is."

"True, and I understand all that. But, Rodney, what about you? Tonight, I mean. What I've been trying to tell you is that if you're staying anywhere near the river yourself, you may be in danger, too. Aren't there more shanties upstream from the old park? I know for a fact there are quite a few near the East Street Bridge right now. Beyond there, I'm not sure. The Coast Guard will certainly go after those tied up by the bridge. And they'll likely do it even if the people in those shanties have already been scared away by what happened today. By now I would think they must have been. Still, the authorities will more than likely sink their boats or set them on fire. No sense in sinking some and leaving others. So, what I'm saying, Rodney, is stay here, please. Protect yourself."

"I appreciate your concern, Delia, and your offer. You've been awfully good to me, but I should go. I'll be all right. I've even had nightmares about just such an attack. But the place where I stay is very well concealed, as Dale can tell you. Jingle and I can barely find it ourselves when we go there after dark. I will leave Jingle with you and Sammy, however, since you asked, but as for me, I'm not staying."

"Then you're forcing me to confess something I've been keeping to myself all this time—I do know where you live." Delia rose from the chair at the dining table and walked slowly to the kitchen sink. There she stood staring out the window for a moment before she turned to them and resumed her story.

"I know that it is a shantyboat, and I know that it's not far from the lumberyard. So, if knowing that puts me in danger, then I'm already in danger up to my neck."

Both Rodney and Dale were dumbfounded for the moment and stood silent, just staring at Delia.

"Dale, I know you told me not to ask about where the two of you lived, that it wasn't safe for me to know, and you were sweet to be so concerned about me. But when you told me that, I already knew. I didn't say so because I didn't want you to worry about me. But last summer, before Sammy and I left for Pittsburgh, I saw the two of you in the lumberyard. I was cleaning Sammy's bedroom and happened to glance across the street, and there you were, both of you, about to cross the lumberyard driveway. I thought maybe the yard was going to open again. I was so happy, so excited to think that. I was even hoping at that moment that soon I could contact Randy and tell him to come home, that there would be work for him again right here. I was still in touch with Walter then, so I intended to ask him about it, just to be sure, before I called Randy and asked him to quit his warehouse job. Those were my first thoughts. Then I saw you taking supplies down the hill, through the back gate. That's when I knew you weren't there because of the yard reopening. I knew it had to be something else you were doing.

"And when, later on, I saw you taking still more supplies out of the sheds and going down the hill with them every time, I decided to investigate. So, one evening after I'd watched you two head for the canteen and shelter, I knew you wouldn't be back until the next morning. I asked Mrs. Sayers next door to watch Sammy for me for a little while. I told her Walter had called and asked me to check to be sure that he'd relocked the lumberyard's rear gate after his last visit. I walked around the yard's fence and went down the hill. It's a long way around there, but I did it. Then I found your partially finished shantyboat. I could tell right away what it was going to be. You had the deck finished and floating on blue barrels, the kind I remembered the yard used for display furring strips and dowels. I recognized those barrels right away. After that, I could have told Walter what I knew, that you were stealing his property, but I didn't."

"And why didn't you?" Rodney asked matter-of-factly.

"Because I could see how desperate you two were. I put myself in your place and thought what I might try to do if I were to lose my house. I'd probably try to do something just like what you two were doing, especially if I had a partner to help me. I could see that you were at least doing something to help yourselves, even if you were stealing the materials to do it. Anyway, I didn't tell Walter anything. If anyone was going to tell him, I thought it should be the guard's place to do it. Besides, not long after finding your half-built shanty,

I took Sammy and left for Pittsburgh to be with Randy for the rest of the summer. By then I had my own problems to deal with."

Dale spoke up now. "And when you returned home, did you see anything then?"

"I did. And I think you know what it was. In October I saw that the stove pipe was missing from outside of Walter's office. I guessed you had taken it, along with Walter's little antique stove, to prepare the shanty for winter. Walter was always so proud of that stove. A few days after that, I heard a loud cry, a painful cry with the fear of death in it. I recognized that it was Walter's voice. And when I looked, I saw him. He was lying at your feet, Rodney. And you, Dale, when you came into the house that first day when I called for you, when we were sitting on the sofa, I saw Walter's watch on your arm."

"And who else knows about this?" Rodney asked, his voice sharp with concern now. "Did you tell anyone?"

"No, don't worry about that. No one else knows. I could have told, of course. And if I had, you would certainly have known that by now. When the Federation authorities were in the yard with Agnes, I could easily have walked across the street and said to them, 'Hey, there, I know why you're here, and I can tell you everything you need to know.' But I didn't. In some ways I wanted to. For the sake of revenge, I wanted to. Because, you see, that was my sugar daddy you killed. That's when I started becoming desperate, seeing Walter collapsed there at your feet, Rodney. And then you, Dale, helping to roll Walter's body down the hill. I saw all that, too.

"Walter was my security in this ugly world. He had always given me money for helping him with the yard's bookkeeping and because he enjoyed flirting with me. When the yard closed, of course, he didn't need my bookkeeping help any more. But after Randy left, he started giving me money again anyway, small amounts here and there while asking me how Randy was doing. He'd stop by the house here every time he visited the yard, maybe once a month. I think he truly felt sorry about the layoffs, as though he had personally let all of you down, even if he didn't tell you that.

"And what's more, it's a good thing he did give me money, because Randy was shorting me. I knew he was even before I went to Pittsburgh to see him. I had checked on how much he was making and could guess how much he needed for his own living expenses.

The difference was too great. Randy had gotten himself a girlfriend there, it turns out. Happens a lot, I suppose. The husband goes off to find work in another town, he's far from home, he's lonely, he meets someone. I'm sure it's happening a lot these days to a lot of families.

"But then what is the wife supposed to do, just sit and wait for him to come to his senses? Just ignore his infidelity? No, at least not me, I didn't. Once I knew for certain about the other woman—you see, Randy was careless with his cell phone—I managed to get access to Randy's bank account. Then I transferred half of it to my account the morning Sammy and I left him. I didn't feel a bit guilty about doing it, either, because, as I said before, I knew he had been shorting me on support since getting his job, or more likely, since getting his mistress. Seems that all the overtime he was supposed to be working was actually time spent with her, even after Sammy and I came to stay with him. And some of the money he earned was spent on her, also. I found out all I needed to know by examining his cell phone while he showered.

"So, I had the money Randy owed me for support, and I still had Walter's help … that is, until I saw him dead at your feet, Rodney, and you, Dale, coming up the hill to help move his body. I decided then and there that somehow you two were going to become my new support. I didn't know how just yet, but I knew I had to find a way. And naturally, I couldn't tell you about what had happened with Randy, because then you wouldn't trust me and we'd never have gotten this business started. So, I deceived you, especially you, Dale. I'm sorry that I did, but I had to. And I'd do it again today."

Dale spoke up now, "So, you've known all along? You knew we killed Walter Badgett, yet you took us in as your employees and took me as your lover, now the father of the baby you're carrying?"

"Yes, I did. As I told you before, desperation sharpens our will to survive, makes us think things we would never think otherwise and do things we'd never dare do before. Just as you two did in killing Walter. But that doesn't mean I don't love you, Dale, because I do and knew I would when I asked you to move in with us. You told me how the workers looked at me when I brought Randy his lunches. Well, I did some looking myself, and I saw you." She rose from the table now and embraced him.

"Then I have a confession, also, Delia," Dale said after kissing her. "Rodney's not the only one who committed a murder. During

143

the summer, while you were gone, we caught a fellow spying on us while we were building our shanty. He had followed us from the canteen that morning. The ground was still wet from a thunderstorm the day before, and this guy slipped along the bank while he was hiding in the shrubbery watching us work on the shanty. He tried to get away, but I caught him and killed him with a hammer. I beat him to death, because I couldn't just let him go and squeal on us. I knew that's what he'd do, and I knew what would happen to us if he did. So, I killed him the only way I could. That's how much the shantyboat meant to us."

Delia pulled a chair from the kitchen table and collapsed onto it, suddenly feeling enormously tired and sad. She put her elbows on the table and her face in her open hands, saying as she did, "We're a fine bunch, aren't we? Killers, liars, and thieves."

Then she raised her head and looked at them, Rodney sitting across from her but still holding Jingle while Dale knelt beside her with his arms around her shoulders. "And I'll be bringing another child into a world such as this, a world in which we've done such things."

Then Rodney added, "Yes, we're killers and liars and thieves but only because we're trying to be free men and women again. And doing all that in a world in which we have much to confess but have no one left to forgive us."

"Can't we forgive each other?" Delia asked.

"Yes, we can, for the things we've done to one another," Rodney replied, "but what does that mean? Does it really count? Is that really absolution for the things we've done to others? Doesn't forgiveness have to come from someone who's sinless to really count?"

After dinner Rodney left for the evening, still saying that he'd be fine and that he wasn't worried, despite his premonitions. Jingle followed him to the door and tried to leave with him, as was their usual practice. Only Sammy's quick work in scooping up Jingle prevented the cat's escape.

After watching Rodney disappear into the dusk, Dale turned to Delia. "We cleared up a lot of things tonight, but you didn't mention anything about what happened to Randy after you and Sammy left. I know you don't like my bringing him up, but I can't help but be curious about him, since I am in his house living with his wife, and she's pregnant with our child. Do you know what has happened to him? Have you still not heard anything from him?"

"Absolutely nothing, just as I told you, and I don't expect to hear anything any more. I didn't lie to you about that, even though I'll admit I was trying hard to make you feel sorry for me. Before Sammy and I left, I wrote him a note telling him that I knew about his mistress and that I had taken the money I thought was rightfully mine. I also told him that he should change his account, at least the password, if he didn't want me to take any more money. And that much I know he did. I checked. After we got back to Parkeston, I've never heard from him again. Not a word. He was probably just as happy to have us gone. No need to send us money any longer. So, he should have quickly recovered what I'd taken. I didn't want to tell you what I'd done because, as I said, I wanted you to feel sorry for me and trust me, sorry enough to accept my business proposal and sorry enough to replace Randy beside me in bed. So, all I can say about him now is that I assume he is still working his job and most likely living with his mistress. Maybe she's joined him in that little efficiency apartment, or maybe he's joined her. So there! Now I've nothing left to confess except to say I'm glad my plan worked out and that you are here with me and not still living in that shantyboat. And I'm glad that we're going to have this child together, I really am, even though I worry about what kind of world it will inherit from us."

Chapter 21: Final Things

The night was warm enough for the windows to be open and for the night sounds to infiltrate their bedroom—coyotes prowling the riverbank, cats squalling in the vacant lot where Rodney had rescued Jingle, lonely dogs everywhere complaining to the full moon and to one another, and owls, recently returned to the town to hunt in its wooded lots, hooting nearby like specters.

Dale looked about the room as he lay beside Delia. He thought of the room now as "their bedroom," and said so routinely to Delia, who would smile at him each time he said it. She smiled at him a lot now that she was pregnant, and he hoped their spate of confessions earlier that evening, especially his own confession of murder, wouldn't put an end to her smiles.

About the time he began to drift into sleep with Delia in her usual position beside him, clutching his left arm at the bicep, he heard bursts of sound, staccato-like, distant but nevertheless distinct. Then the sounds came again, no closer but longer and more pronounced this time. Dale sat upright, trying to decide just what it was and where it was and what, if anything, he should do.

Awakening, as well, Delia released his arm and asked, "What's wrong?"

"That noise," he replied. "Did you hear it?"

"No," she said, and started to say more, but the noise started again, even longer now, though only slightly louder. "Oh, God!" she cried. "Do you think it's the Coast Guard again attacking the other shanties? And they're doing it at night so that no one sees them?"

Dale leaped from the bed wearing only the briefs Delia had bought him. He flew across the room to the window. There he could see, downstream from the lumberyard, the glow of fires reflecting on the river. Too far away for him to see the flames themselves, but the light was bright enough to redden the river valley with flashes of light extending all the way up to the lumberyard.

"What is it, Dale? What do you see?" Delia asked as she joined him by the window and whispered to him in order not to awaken Sammy. She wore her summer weight nightgown now and carried the bathrobe Dale had neglected in his haste to put on, a bathrobe left behind by Randy. She draped it about his shoulders and then clung to him as he continued to look out the window at the blazing fires, all but ignoring her for the moment.

"You must be right about the Coast Guard coming back," Dale finally said as he worked his arms through the sleeves of the robe while still watching the river. "Just look!"

When Delia looked out the window, the noise started up again, and the lights quickly grew brighter with flashes of color—reds and yellows and blues—as though some new combustions or explosions were occurring.

"That's what it is. The Coast Guard is attacking the shanties by the East Street Bridge. And look, Dale, now there's a speedboat coming this way, coming up the river!"

Dale could see the boat heading swiftly upstream, led by the beam of its searchlight. "It's going in Rodney's direction!" he exclaimed.

The boat quickly passed out of sight behind the lumberyard's storage sheds, but they could hear its motor slow and then stop. Occasionally, the distinct probing beam of its searchlight was visible through the trees along the riverbank.

"Oh, no, I think they've found our shanty!" Dale exclaimed. "It sounds like they've stopped in about the right place."

Then came the sound of the speedboat's machine gun, a long burst followed by several shorter ones. Dale looked away for a moment in fear of what he might see, but then, courage renewed, glimpsed out the window again. Now he could see a new light, a fire flickering at first. Filtering up from the woods along the river, it was growing increasingly brighter even while the beam of the searchlight moved about among the trees. The fire began moving slowly and eerily downstream. Soon, it was passing behind the lumberyard and out of direct sight propelled, it seemed, only by the river's steady flow, and creating as it went a glow on the water against which the trees along the riverbank appeared as graceful, leafy silhouettes. Then the light disappeared behind the sheds in the yard, then reappeared again, this time in the expanse of the river visible from Delia's house from which just moments before they had seen the Coast Guard speedboat approaching. This area was already alight with the fires farther downstream when this new object floated into view.

"That's our shantyboat, all right!" Dale exclaimed. He immediately turned away from Delia, threw off his robe, and began to dress.

"What are you doing?" Delia was frantic. "Where are you going?"

"To see if I can find Dale. He might be hurt!"

"But the speedboat is still up that way. It hasn't come back down the river. You could be walking right into danger, Dale! Don't go! Please don't go!"

"But he's my friend. I have to go. He needs me." Dressed now, Dale hurried down the stairs with Delia right behind him, her untied nightgown flowing and fluttering out around her nakedness.

At the front door she grabbed his arm before he could open it. "You can't leave me, Dale. You just can't." She was emphatic. "If you get killed or even injured, we'd lose everything. Don't you see that? You can't go."

He hesitated, with her hand touching his, both hands on the doorknob. He looked at her now with her nightgown still open and her swollen abdomen exposed to him.

Delia tied her nightgown's sash around her waist and then resumed her plea. "If Rodney were still on the shantyboat, he's dead by now. But surely he's not. He's bound to have heard the shooting down at East Street and heard the speedboat headed toward him, bound to have seen its searchlight, too. Noise bounces up and down this river valley as though it's shouted from a megaphone. So, if we heard it all the way up here, he surely heard it, as well, and had time to escape. Remember, he said he had a premonition about this very thing. I'm sure he knows what to do."

"But we don't know that for certain."

"Dale, don't go. I'm begging you. You have no good reason to go and every reason to stay."

"But what about Rodney? He was my friend, the best friend I've ever had."

"And what about me? I won't be abandoned again. I won't be. Besides, we both have this baby to worry about now." Delia grabbed Dale's hand and placed it on her abdomen, making him feel it through her sheer nightgown. "And besides, there's nothing you can do for him now. If he was still on that shantyboat, he's dead by now. And if he wasn't, he knows very well how to get here, and he will.

He'll come soon. He's bound to, so just wait." With that, Delia snapped on the porch light.

Then they heard the tinkle of Jingle's collar bell. A moment later Sammy came shuffling down the stairs, finally awakened by all the desperate talking. Jingle followed him and immediately took up a post by the front door, looking at it, waiting expectantly for it to open and Rodney to walk in.

"What is it, Mom? Why are you guys down here talking?" Sammy asked when he reached the bottom of the stairs.

"There was a boat on the river, honey. It was on fire, but it's drifted out of sight now," Delia said, then looked out the window again. "We were wondering if it was Mr. Tanner's boat. He and Jingle have been living on a shantyboat."

"Living on a boat? Really? That sounds like fun." Sammy's arrival and his excitement helped cut the tension between Dale and Delia. "Mr. Tanner had a boat, Jingle," Sammy said as he knelt to pet the cat, "and you lived on it, too. I didn't know that. But where is Mr. Tanner now, Mom?"

"We're not sure, Sammy. That's why we're up and looking out the window. It's a good thing Jingle stayed with you tonight."

Then Dale spoke up, "Look! Someone's coming down the street."

"Is it Rodney?" Delia asked.

"Can't tell yet, but the person is tall, so could be. Looks to be carrying something, too. And he's still coming this way!"

A few minutes more and Rodney was climbing the steps to Delia's house. Dale flung the door open for him and stepped onto the porch. "Are you all right? We heard shooting."

As Rodney stepped inside, Jingle attached himself to Rodney's pant leg, demanding attention. And so, Rodney delayed his reply long enough to pick up Jingle. "Good thing you stayed here tonight, little fellow," he said to the cat and rubbed cheeks with it before turning back to Dale. "Yes, I'm fine ... but just barely. Our shanty was shot up and torched. I was lucky to escape. Even after setting the shanty on fire, the Coast Guardsmen shined their searchlight all along the riverbank and fired off a few rounds whenever they thought they saw something. Fortunately, none of those somethings was me! I was well up the hill by that time."

149

As Dale and Rodney talked, Delia collected Jingle and turned him over to Sammy, and then sent them both back to bed.

"Yes, we were worried when we saw the Coast Guard headed your way," Dale said. "And then we saw the shanty floating downstream, on fire. So, how did you escape?"

"Oh, I heard the noise of the attack they were making, most likely down by the East Street Bridge, just as you predicted, Delia. And soon after that, I could see the light from the fires on the shanties. I remembered what you said about the possibility of more attacks, Delia, as well as what I had experienced in my dreams. So, I thought, 'I better get the hell out of here while the getting is good, just in case they have come up the river looking for more shanties.' That's when I grabbed these clothes you bought me and the extra pair of shoes I'd been saving." Rodney was still holding them in a bundle. "Then out the door of our shanty I went, across the plank and up the riverbank as fast as I could go without falling. When I got to where I thought they wouldn't be able to see me, I hid behind some trees and waited, just to see what they were going to do. In no time, the searchlight was focused on the shanty, and the speedboat pulled alongside it. In a few moments more, machine gun bullets were tearing through what we'd worked most of the summer and fall to build. I could see the wood chips flying up into the spotlight's beam and could hear the cabin windows shattering. Then someone on the speedboat lit a torch and tossed it into the cabin, right through the broken window, it looked like. The bedding caught fire first. Soon after that, the entire shanty went up in flames. I stayed put while they used the searchlight to check along the riverbank. Finally, the speedboat moved further upstream but not very far. By that time, I knew it was impossible for me to put out the fire on the shanty. Still, I couldn't help but watch it for a while. So much of Dale and me were in that shanty. Before long, though, the fire burned through the shanty's mooring lines, and it started to drift downstream in full blaze. I guess that's when you saw it. After that, I headed on up here before the Coast Guard speedboat returned. All that work, Dale, the whole summer we spent on it, and now it's gone in a flash."

"That's a shame, Rodney," Delia was quick to say, "but at least you escaped. And you know you can stay here as long as you need to—until you find a place of your own. No need to go back to life in the shelters and canteens. Not after all you've been through already.

Besides, you have a job to do each day. And I have plenty of work lined up for the two of you as soon as dawn breaks."

"Thank you, Delia. You've been an angel through this whole mess. Perhaps more properly, I should say you've been our Athena, since you've been so wise and so practical and providential."

"Well, I doubt that Randy would agree with you if he were standing here, not about either assessment—angel or Athena. But that's his problem ... that is, if he even still thinks about me at all. Either way, he's not my problem any more. My job is to encourage the two of you. Didn't Athena do that for the heroes of Athens?"

"She did, indeed," Rodney replied. "In fact, I think that was her main job. She also guided the city's politicians. Too bad you can't do that here, as well."

"Although Randy may not think of you, Delia, I can say for sure that I do," Dale said as he embraced her. "But you know what?"

"What?" she asked, kissing him quickly.

"It's almost three o'clock. If we're going to get any sleep at all and be fit for work tomorrow—today, actually—we better get back into bed."

"But before we do," Rodney said, "step back out on the porch for a minute and take a look around. You probably didn't notice this before because your own porch light was on, but I noticed this right away as I was walking down here from the river. Especially once I got up onto Camden Avenue, I could see it."

"What is it?" Delia asked.

"Come out here and take a look for yourselves, both of you."

After Delia and Dale followed Rodney onto the porch, they could see all up and down the street that porch lights were on, spaced apart in some places, it was true, by the vacant lots or abandoned houses, but enough turned on to light up the street in both directions.

"And just look across the river to the other side of town," Rodney said, pointing with a sweeping motion as if to take in the entire town. Across the way they saw a multitude of lights, as well, spreading up from the river to the communities on the hills surrounding Parkeston.

"Should be nothing on but the streetlights at this time of the night," Rodney said. "That and the lights of a few midnight owls, perhaps. But no! Just look, look everywhere! People are saying something right now. They're saying, 'We know what you did,

151

Federation. We know you came in the night to kill some of us who have resisted you. You came in the night so that no radio station would report on you this time, but we heard you, and we know what you did, and now we're telling you and each other that we won't forget it. And we'll resist you from now on!' "

"Oh, look toward downtown," Delia said, gesturing now in that direction. "Even lights down that way are coming on. You wouldn't think there would be anyone down there at this time of the night to turn on a light. This is really remarkable, all the more so because it's happening in the middle of the night. Someone has to be deliberately doing that."

Rodney added, "I think a lot of people must have heard that same radio broadcast you heard, Delia, or at least heard about it. I think it has to be more than the noise tonight that got them up. Some of these lights are way too far from the river for those people to have heard anything. And more are still coming on."

Then Dale added, "The whole town's gradually lighting up."

"Yes, I see that," Delia said. "People must be calling one another and asking them to turn on their lights. It looks like a spontaneous demonstration. Soon, the entire town is going to be lit up."

Rodney put his hands on the porch banister to steady himself as he leaned forward to survey first the river scene and then to look up and down Camden Avenue. Next, he walked to the far end of the porch, the side adjacent to Pineview, and looked up the street. "There are lights on up this way, too," he reported, pointing. "Just imagine, a freedom revolt starting here in our little town, all over shantyboats." Then he looked at Delia. "Freedom boats some of us killed for, as you now know."

"Yes, I do know," she replied as she and Dale joined him to look up Pinecrest Street.

"But if we had only thought of a way to provide some kind of service, the way you have, Delia, all that could have been avoided. Instead, Dale and I only thought about ourselves, our need for freedom and not how we could help people with their needs as you have done. And our way of responding to this crisis turned into tragedy. But what you've got us involved in now has a future, one that can build on itself. It's that little bit of slack in the coils around us that the Federation python has allowed, either through its own

152

neglect or perhaps even allowed deliberately, as you suggested, because it sees that its economic policies aren't working but won't admit that. And now here we are, using that slack in the coils to our advantage. Soon, the Federation will need to loosen its coils even more, just to keep people from revolting as they've shown tonight they can do, and so on and so on. And hopefully, we'll gradually recover our freedoms just the way we lost them—one by one, a little at a time. At least, that's my hope, that this is just the beginning."

"I agree," Dale said. "I can see that happening as sure as dawn is coming."

"Well, I'm glad you both think so," Delia said. "But we all better get back to bed for what's left of the night, because come that dawn, Athena is going to fling you heroes onto the street to renew our little revolution."

With that, they went inside and closed the door on the night. But they left the porch light on along with all the others, even as the fires from the shantyboats died out.

About the Author

Carl Parsons, a former plant manager for TRW Automotive, has had a secondary career as a college instructor of rhetoric and literature. He has a BA and MA in English from West Virginia University; doctoral course work completed at the University of Pittsburgh, and a MS in Manufacturing Management from Kettering University. Born in Parkersburg, WV, he now resides in Kodak, TN, near Knoxville.

Milton Keynes UK
Ingram Content Group UK Ltd.
UKHW011106201123
432908UK00007B/1272